Another Chance

This book is a work of fiction caused by my vivid imagination. All names, characters, events, places, products etc. have been used for this fictional purpose. If, by chance, they or it resembles someone or something; living or dead, it is by coincidence.

***** Although this is Christian Fiction, there is some foul language included.**

Published by: Twins Write 2 Publishing

This book is licensed for your enjoyment only. This Book may not be resold or given to others. If you would like to share this book, please purchase an additional copy for each person you share it with. If you're reading this book and you did not purchase it, or it was not purchased for your use, then you should return to Amazon and purchase your own copy. Thank you for respecting my work as an author.

Dedication

This book is dedicated to those of you who think love will never find you. It will. How do I know? Because you deserve to be loved and God will send you the person meant for you. All you have to do is trust Him and His timing.

My Thanks

I'll always begin by thanking God. It was Him who believed enough in who He created to keep calling. Even the many times I ignored Him, He never gave up. This is why I never give up and I proudly and unapologetically serve and worship Him.

To my family; my husbae Willie, children, mom, sisters, brothers—the entire family; know that I love each of you for supporting me, release after release.

A special shout out to my sister Laquisha and my girl, Shakendria who willingly help me to ensure I craft great books. To each of you who support Lakisha, the PreacHER, Author and Blogger … THANK YOU! I wouldn't be who I am without supporters like you who purchase, download, recommend and review my books. Please, don't stop believing in me.

Another Chance

When you close your heart to love, but God doesn't

Chapter 1

September 2019

"Members of St. Joseph, we are pleased, honored and excited to welcome our new elected leader Pastor Jeffrey Walker and his fiancé Chance McGhee." Darryl Latham, head of the deacon board announces. "We are looking forward to more of those fiery sermons and who knows maybe we'll get to hear Lady McGhee, soon to be Walker, sing too."

I look out over the congregation with a huge smile. Although my stomach is in knots, this is what Jeff has been preparing for since I met him three years ago. I begin to think how much my life is about to change as First Lady of a church.

He tugs on my hand, pulling me from my thoughts. I smile and wave before taking my seat as he walks to the podium.

"I did it," he beams after the service is over. "Wow, I can't believe I'm finally senior pastor."

"I'm very proud of you."

"Man, I cannot wait to make some changes. This is a cool church, but it can be so much better," he says excitedly opening the drawers of the desk.

"Babe, don't you think you need to take things slow? You were just voted in."

"Right, I was," he asserts, "which means they trust me and my vision."

"Oh, just you?"

"Chance, you know what I meant," he waves his hands.

"I'm only offering advice. You don't need to move too fast and get in over your head."

I understand," he walks over and grabs my shoulders, "but you don't have to worry about me. I know exactly what I'm doing. And I guess you can sing for them a couple of Sundays, but I don't want you joining the choir or trying to lead worship."

"Why not?" I ask crossing my arms. "It's what I did before I met you. In fact, it was what I was doing when I met you."

"Keyword, before. You don't need to do it anymore. Now, don't kill the vibe because we have another two hours of smiling and mingling at this celebration dinner in the fellowship hall."

"I'm not killing the vibe, but I want to keep my identity which is more than just your wife and first lady. I'm a worshipper Jeff. You know this."

"We'll talk about it later," he quickly dismisses the conversation turning to walk out.

"I can't do this anymore," Jeff says from the bathroom.

"Do what?" I ask walking to the door unfastening my shirt.

He rinses his toothbrush and turns toward me.

"This relationship. Us."

I laugh but abruptly stop when I realize he isn't joking.

"Chance look—"

"Please don't pacify me Jeff. What is going on?"

He sighs, leaning against the sink. "I'm not happy anymore. I've tried to be but I'm not and I don't know what else to do."

"Seriously, you're joking, right?"

"No," he states wiping his face. "I've been giving this a lot of thought and Chay baby, I'm sorry but I'm just not happy with you anymore. I know this is hard to hear and you're going to be upset, but it's time I was honest."

"Wow, after three years you're just figuring this out? You didn't know this six months ago before you proposed, and we started making plans for a wedding that's in three months. Not before we agreed to this freaking vacation in two weeks with my family. Yet, magically you "figured out" you're not happy now?"

He lays the towel down and walks over to me. "It's not like you're making it seem. Yes, I knew a while ago and I've been trying to figure out a way to tell you and now seemed like the perfect time. You know, instead of leaving you at the altar. Baby, I never meant to hurt you."

"Stop lying, and please quit calling me baby," I yell. "You meant to do this, and you knew it would hurt me, so miss me with this. Tell me something, did you string me along until you became the pastor of St. Joseph?"

"No, this has nothing to do with the church."

I laugh. "Right. It's mighty funny since you've been installed, I decorated your office all nice, you've received the keys and the parking space you're calling the wedding off. Yeah, this has everything to do with the church. God, I knew it," I yell. "You've been making a fool of me for three years."

My skin begins to heat from the anger coursing through my body and I want to break something. I'm walking around in a circle as tears fall.

"Chance don't cry. Baby, I'm sorry. Please don't cry."

"Dude, these tears are the only thing keeping me from bashing your head in." I begin to walk out the bedroom but quickly turn back to him. He jumps. "You know I don't normally curse but fuck you. We've been together three got damn years and all of a sudden you aren't happy. Here's your happy motherfucker." I say holding up my middle finger. "Talking about, better than leaving you at the altar," I mock, "like I'm a freaking poinsettia at Christmas."

"Chance, I'm sorry."

"Yes, you're very sorry. For three years, I've given you all of me and in a matter of moments, you decide you're not happy. For three years, I've played the perfect First Lady while you interviewed at church after church. I changed the way I dressed to appease you. I don't post as much on social media or hang out with my friends because I wanted to make sure you got everything you desired. Hospital visits, Bible studies, Sunday schools and the many sermons I've had to help you write and this is what I get in return. I even stopped singing for you. But you know what, I don't blame you."

"Chance—"

"I wasn't done," I fume walking closer to him. "No, I don't blame you, this is all on me because I allowed you to change me. I allowed you to use me. I allowed myself to shrink back while you became this great man

of God. I was everything I thought you needed when I knew in my heart it wasn't," I begin to get angry at myself. "God showed me signs and I ignored them, stupidly listening to my flesh and thinking this was love. You even convinced me that He'd sent you to be the head of this house. Like a dummy I fell in line because I thought you had the ear of God. Mane," I hit the inside of my hand with a fist, "I allowed you to become my small g god and—God, forgive me. God, please forgive me and thank you for severing this relationship because I couldn't see it was stunting my growth."

"Chance, will you stop with the dramatics. You know it wasn't like that. I just realized I need something better now that I'm senior pastor of a church."

"Someone," I correct. "You mean someone, right?"

"Well," he looks down.

"That's okay, your words can't hurt me no more than they have. You just remember everything you've said when the better you're searching for can't compare to me. Now, pack the few things you have here, leave my key, block my number and unfriend me on every social media site."

"No, wait," he rushes over to me. "Look, I know I have no right to ask this, but I need us to come up with a way to tell the deacons of St. Joseph."

"Oh, so there's an "us" when it's convenient?"

He sighs looking up to the ceiling. "Can you tell them you're the reason we can't go through with the marriage? Please and this will be the last thing I'll ask of you. If it looks like you called things off, they won't hold it against me."

I stare at him as he clasps his hands together to silently beg.

"You know what, yeah, I'll do this last thing for you."

"Thank you, thank you," he jumps up and down. "We can meet with them tomorrow during the deacon's meeting. I'll pick you up."

"Sounds great, but I'll drive myself."

Chapter 2

I walk into the living room, connect my Bluetooth and blast 'Without You,' by Fantasia.

"Fake, fake, fakin' shit will kill you, boy I know the real you. Really gon' make me expose you for exactly what you are. And I'm feeling a little wavy so right now I don't mind pulling your card," I sing walking into the kitchen to pour me a glass of Stella Rosa Black wine.

Walking back to the living room, he comes down the hall with his bag.

"Chance," he shouts over the music and I ignore him while changing the song to 'Heard it All Before' by Sunshine Anderson. I see him in my peripheral shaking his head and walking off. I sit as he makes a few trips to his car.

"Chance, I'm sorry," he says.

I turn the music down.

"Jeff, just go."

"What about the trip?" he asks.

"What about it?"

"Since the tickets are already paid for, maybe we can go—"

"Dude, if you think I am about to spend five days in Jamaica with your rusty behind and my family, you've lost the small amount of brain cells you manage not to burn away. I'd rather sweep the entire neighborhood with a toothbrush than to go anywhere else with you."

"I've already taken the days off and started to pack. Will you at least think about it? It'll show the deacons there's no ill will between us and it'll give time for the news of our break-up to die down."

"No, you know what can die? You. You act like you're some big named celebrity. Dude, you're a newly elected pastor of a church with maybe two hundred members. Nobody knows you, so get over yourself and get out of my house."

"Hold on, I get you're upset but this is overreacting. I'm the one who paid for this trip."

"You were," I say standing, "however, I'm the one who booked it under my name and with my card so," I shrug and throw him the deuces.

He shakes his head and begins to walk off.

"Jeff, wait."

He turns back with a smile.

"My key," I say holding out my hand.

He pulls his keys from his pocket, fumbling with the ring until he gets it off and slapping it into my hand.

"God bless you," I smirk.

Once he's gone, I change the code on the garage panel and my alarm system. Getting back to the living room, I grab my phone and log into Facebook.

"What's on your mind? I'll tell you what's on my mind Facebook," I say out loud to myself. "These no-good Negroes who think they can play with women's minds and hearts. Can you tell the deacons this was your idea?" I imitate. "Sure. Why not and let Chance continue to be a fool for Jeffrey Walker. Not anymore boo-boo."

I begin to make a post.

#longpost I've made a mistake. I believed God had sent me a man, one who loved and feared Him as much as I did. What I realize now, I was looking through the lenses of lust and not love. When he proposed, I quickly said yes before praying to God to ensure he was the one. Why wouldn't he be, though? He's a minister, educated, handsome with no drama and he said he loved me. This has to be God, doesn't it? I can admit I was wrong because tonight, the man I'm supposed to marry in two months told me he didn't love me anymore. He needs something better. I.E. someone.

Hold on, that's not the worse part. He had the nerve to ask me to lie and say I called the wedding off to save face with the church. I will NOT! God, I wish I'd

been the one to call it off. Maybe then it wouldn't hurt as much to know the man I've changed my entire way of being for could cast me aside like I'm an old pair of shoes that no longer fit.

Sad part, it took him saying those words for me to realize I'd stopped focusing on God. I even put this man before God because he was going to be my husband, the one I'm supposed to submit to. Boy, I was wrong. Not anymore. From now on, I'm loving Chance and before I submit to another man, it'll be on God's authority. God will literally have to put him in my way, sit him next to me or drop him from the sky before I say yes again.

I shared all of this to say, ladies don't ever decrease your worth for a man. If he can't recognize the glory you carry and the value you add to his life, drop his ass. As for me, I'm going to take a moment and cry, then I'll get myself together because I'm a thick, cute, smart, educated woman who can cook, sing, do my own hair and nails and I'm not materialistic. I'm also headed to Jamaica, the trip he paid for, alone.

Oh, if you haven't figured it out by now, the wedding to the newly elected Pastor of St. Joseph Baptist Church, Jeffrey Walker, is OFF.

Y'all be easy. —Chance

I change my status to single and don't bother to block him yet because he's tagged in the post. I log off and go about deleting Jeff's number. Three minutes later, my phone begins to vibrate with calls from my mom and sister.

"That was fast," I say ignoring them. Then Jeff. I ignore him too. He sends a text.

+1 (901) 873-1292: Really Chance? Why would you do that?

+1 (901) 873-1292: I thought we agreed.

+1 (901) 873-1292: Do you know how you've made me look?

+1 (901) 873-1292: Baby, please take it down.

I pick up my glass to refill it. Getting back to my phone, I have thirteen additional messages from Jeff, each getting angrier.

+1 (901) 873-1292: You know what? I was trying to spare your feelings, but you aren't wife material. All your good for is taking care of a man. You'll never find anybody else. <cow emoji>

Me: I've been called worse by far better. Good luck with the deacons. Maybe they won't realize I was the one writing your sermons when you preach Sunday. And it's you're, not your. <finger sign emoji>

I block his number and a few seconds later, I burst into tears.

"God, is this what I deserve?"

Chapter 3

I wake up to banging on my door. I look at the clock and groan. Picking up my phone I see 47 missed calls from Jeff.

The banging continues.

I slowly get out of bed and go into the bathroom.

The banging continues.

I take a shower, brush my teeth, wash my face and pull my locs up into a bun. I take my time getting dressed as there's more banging on the door. Walking into the kitchen, I get a cup from the cabinet and prepare my coffee.

Another loud knock.

Exhaling, I unarm the alarm and snatch the door open.

"Dude, get off my porch."

"Chance, why would you do that?"

"What's wrong with you, Mr. I Need Better?" I smile.

"This isn't funny. You said you'd talk to the deacon board with me," he says with tears in his eyes.

"I did, didn't I? Well, I changed my mind because I felt like I needed something better. Funny how that works, huh?"

"I know what I did was messed up but come on Chance," he sternly states. "This can ruin everything I've worked for. Please baby. Take the post down and come with me to speak to the board at St. Joseph."

"Dude, leave my house."

"That's all I'm asking of you. This one thing," he yells. "Please do this for me."

"Hell no. I'm tired of doing things for you. The last three years, I did more than I should have. I cooked, cleaned, rode your small penis—"

"My what?" he exclaims.

"You heard me, and not once did I complain when you couldn't even give me a decent orgasm. I guess that's what I get for having sex before marriage. Yet, I played the good girl, doing wife stuff thinking that's what you saw in me when the entire time I was only a company keeper."

"It wasn't like that and you know it."

"No, what I know is I allowed you to make a fool of me, not because of low self-esteem, I love all 190 plus pounds of me, yet I surrendered to you thinking you could handle the position of who and what I needed. Truth is, you were too little to ride this ride anyway, however I made exceptions for you. Not anymore. You got me once, you won't ever get the chance to do it again. Goodbye."

His body stiffens. "You're really going to be a low-down bitch about this?" he belittles. "After all I've done for you?"

"There he is, the real Jeffrey Walker. Boo, I'm not surprised you'd call me out my name, that's what simple minded people resort to when they can't hurt you any other way. However, do me a favor and name them."

"Name what?"

"Name what you've done for me, I'll wait." I cross my arms.

He looks around the front of my house.

"I bought that purse," he points, and I go over, empty everything out and give it to him.

"What else?"

"Um," he thinks. "I've taken you out to eat, bought you clothes and shoes."

I laugh. "Yeah, that's all you could do. You couldn't even get a car in your name until I helped you fix your credit, can't put together a decent sermon if your life depended on it and you got the gall to guilt me into keeping your reputation intact. I think not. So, do us both a favor and get out of my house. The one that's in my name and I pay the mortgage on."

"You think you've won but I will not stop until I destroy you in the church circle and social media. By the time I'm done, you won't be able to step foot in St. Joseph or any church again as a member let alone a worship leader. The only singing you'll do from this point on is in the shower."

"Good luck with that."

He walks out the door.

"Jeff, just so you know, I had no plans on going back to St. Joseph anyway. They're too stuck up for me. However, a word of advice, be careful the lies you tell because they can come back to bite you."

For an entire week, there have been post after post about me on social media. I know it's a few of Jeff's family members and friends trying to get a reaction from me. I have so many people sending me screenshots and text messages, but I can care less. He thinks because the church decided to keep him on, he's doing something grand. He isn't. In fact, his first sermon after dumping me was so dry and boring, a man was seen sleep on their live broadcast.

As for me, I'm headed to Jamaica by myself.

I walk onto the plane to find my seat. Reaching it, I put my carry on in the overhead and keep my smaller bag as I slide into the window seat. I connect my headphones and start my music while the plane continues to board. I fasten my seatbelt, close my eyes and lay my head back.

A few minutes later someone bump my arm. I open my eyes to see a man standing there.

"My apologies, did you say something?" I ask taking out my headphones.

"No, I should be the one apologizing. I didn't mean to wake you. I was trying not to bump you and ended up doing it anyway."

"It's no problem, I wasn't asleep. Chance," I say extending my hand.

He pauses before taking it. "Mason," he stutters.

"It's nice to meet you Mason."

He takes the aisle seat and I am praying no one is on standby to get the seat that would have been Jeff's. After being on the phone with the airline, explaining the situation, I was able to turn his ticket into a credit for a future flight. I put my headphones back in and begin my preflight meditation.

Two hours in, I finally take off my headphones and put my bag in the middle seat before stretching my arms. I excuse myself and go to the bathroom. Getting back to my seat, I turn my phone off airplane mode and it begins to vibrate nonstop.

"Wow, someone is really trying to reach you." Mason says.

"Yeah well, he can try on." I say deleting the voicemails and texts from Jeff before putting this new number on block.

"Old boyfriend."

"Something like that. Can I ask you a question Mason?"

"Sure," he replies sipping on his drink.

"Are all men assholes?"

Chapter 4

He gets choked. After he is done coughing, he begins to laugh.

"I wasn't expecting that, but to answer your question, no. Men aren't assholes, boys are."

"Well, I just spent three years in a relationship wasting time with a boy I thought would be my husband. He decided, two weeks ago, he was no longer happy in our relationship. The worst part, it was after I'd put my all into making him into who he is."

"You don't have to explain, I get it. Sad reality, this kind of thing happens more than we care to admit. Even after seeing the signs flashing bright red, we still go full steam ahead thinking we can change what we did not create."

"True. I never thought he'd turn into that person though."

"Yes, you did," he boldly states, and I raise my eyebrow at him. "I ask this in Godly love, but how many times has he let you down before, but you kept making excuses for him?"

His question sting, and it instantly makes me feel a type of way, so I face the window.

He touches my arm. "I didn't mean to upset you. I'll say this, and I'm done. Many times, we focus on the potential of a person and not the purpose of the relationship in which we've joined together for. Potential is the capacity to become or develop into something in the future, when purpose is the reason for which something exists. It's evident this man wasn't part of your purpose, but he's what God used for you to see the potential in who you're destined to be in the future."

I wipe the tears falling.

"Ms. Chance," he turns my face to him, "that man didn't have the capacity to handle the thing God has ordained for your life and sometimes the severing has to hurt to keep you from going back. You're meant to be a wife, not a placeholder and don't allow him to be the reason you close yourself off to love."

"Thank you for being honest with me," I tell him. "Are you a therapist?"

"You can say that. Excuse me for a moment," he says grabbing his phone and getting up.

He gets back and for a few minutes we don't talk.

"Chance, I apologize for overstepping. I have no right to pry into your life and by no means do I know the ins and outs of your relationship. Please, I hope you can accept my apology."

"No Mason, you were right. I did see the signs and I should have dumped him a long time ago, but I was worried about my family and not my true happiness. Now, I have to face their judgmental looks during our annual family trip which happens to coincide with my birthday and Thanksgiving."

"At least you'll be in beautiful Jamaica."

"You haven't met my family," I laugh.

"This is the last thing I will say and then I'll leave you alone."

"Ok, I'm ready." I say acting like I am bracing myself.

He laughs. "Men will do what you allow and accept. This doesn't mean you have to create a list of unattainable standards, but it means sitting down together and seeing what level you're both on. Having an open and honest talk, in the beginning, can cut out some of the hurt on the backend. And even if the conversation goes the way you hope, reevaluate it every once in a while."

"Why is that?"

"To be sure you and that person are still on the same level."

"I never thought of that."

"Anyway, I've done enough counseling."

"Oh no, it's been great and well needed. Thank you."

"No, thank you for listening. It allowed me to get my mind off of traveling alone."

"Tell me about it."

He nods.

"No really, tell me about it. You've heard all my issues so it's only right you tell me yours." I laugh.

"Well," he says clearing his throat. "This was supposed to be a vacation with my wife. We purchased it a year ago, but little did we know, she wouldn't be here to enjoy it. She died nine months ago."

"I am so sorry."

"Don't be because she's now enjoying a rest, we all hope to one day get and I wouldn't wish her back to this world. After watching her health decline, there's no way I could ask God to keep her here."

"How long were you married? If you don't mind me asking."

"I was blessed to be able to spend 19 years with her. We grew up together and, in some way, I believe it prepared me to live without her."

"How?"

"The night she died, I was sitting with her in the temporary hospital room, in our home and God allowed me to see all the things He'd done over the course of her illness and our life to make me ready. We took pictures, had date nights, took trips and created memories. I found out after she'd passed that she made videos. The best part, she got the chance to tell me goodnight."

By now, I can't even hide my tears. He looks at me and smiles before handing me his napkin.

"Before she slept away, I thought my heart would be shattered beyond repair, but it wasn't. It hurt, don't get me wrong yet knowing I got the chance to experience her and the love she had for me, was comfort enough to not fall to pieces. It was her loving me that will one day allow me to love someone else, properly."

"Wow," I say wiping my face. "I hope to one day experience that. Right now, I find myself being angry at God and love. I know He isn't to blame when this was my own stupidity, but I wish He would have woken me up before I wasted three years."

"You wouldn't have seen it then and this is why we have to trust God's timing. Don't look at it as time wasted, it was a lesson learned. See, God gives us the space to make mistakes, because they either grow us or they hinder us. We have to choose which."

"I know, it still doesn't take away the hurt of being made a fool of."

"You aren't a fool, we make foolish decisions but that's due to this fleshly body. See, you have to guard your heart above everything else because Solomon says in Proverbs four and twenty-three, it'll determine the course of your life. Trust me, well try to trust me when I say," he laughs, "you'll find love again, if you give it another chance. Next time, put a password on your heart that only God has and make him go through God to get it."

"What do you do?" I ask him.

He opens his mouth at the same time the flight attendant interrupts with landing instructions.

"Ms. Chance, it was so nice to meet and talk to you. Maybe I'll see you around and you'd allow me to take you to dinner."

"I'd like that."

"Are you from Memphis?"

"I am."

"I would love it if you would visit my church sometime," he says handing me a card.

"A pastor, I should have known." I say my mood changing. "My ex is also a pastor. He was recently appointed to St. Joseph Baptist Church."

"Jeffrey Walker, makes sense," he chuckles.

"You know him?"

"I think everybody does after the live video of his sleeping member went viral," he laughs again. "I'm sorry, I shouldn't be laughing."

"Oh, you aren't hurting me. I'm only glad I'm free from that."

"Chance, thank you for allowing me to pry into your business. I promise I'm not always like this and I pray it won't stop you from visiting us one Sunday."

"It hasn't and thank you."

Chapter 5

Mason and I are staying in the same resort, so we take the shuttle from the airport. Making it to the hotel, we part ways at check in.

"Will you need more than two keys, Mrs. Walker," the young lady asks.

"Actually, it's Ms. McGhee and no, only one. It's just me."

"Oh, the reservation is booked for you and a Mr. Walker."

"Not anymore," I give her a fake smile as to hurry up.

"No problem," she nods.

She finally hands me the key, motioning for a bellhop to help with my bags.

"Dang, you could answer your phone." I roll my eyes at the sound of my sister's voice behind me. I take a deep breath and face her.

"What's up Taylor?"

"I thought you'd be a ball of mess by now. I must say you're stronger than I thought," she chuckles. "Ain't no way I would have shown up after getting dumped again."

"Why wouldn't I? This trip was already booked and paid for. It's also my vacation."

"Paid for by a man who dumped you. Girl, we knew that boy would never go through with marrying you. Everybody could see he was only using you. Except you," she shakes her head.

"Why is that Taylor?"

"Because you're naïve. I'm sorry to be so blunt, but maybe if you lost fifty pounds, you'll be more appealing to a man."

I hear the bellhop suck in his breath as the elevator opens. I wait until the people get off, grab my small bag and follow the young man inside.

"You can act like you didn't hear me, but we have five days together and I got a lot more to say," she laughs. "Shoot, it isn't my fault you got the genes from dad's side of the family. Let me move to give you room."

She laughs until I continue stepping back pressing her into the wall.

"Chance," she pushes, "move, I can't breathe."

The elevator reaches the eleventh floor and the doors open.

"After you," I tell the bellhop.

"You're wrong for that," Taylor pants once we're out.

"Yeah well, in your words, we have five days together and I got more to say and do. Please don't try me." I walk off leaving her standing there.

Later that night

"Chance, aren't you ready yet?"

"Yes mom, I'm coming." I yell in response regretting letting her into my room.

"Finally," she says when I walk out the bathroom. "It took you all this time to put on that."

I roll my eyes. "I told you not to wait."

"Well, someone had too otherwise you probably wouldn't show up to dinner."

"Can we please not do this tonight?"

She holds the door open and I shake my head as I grab my purse. We walk to the restaurant to meet my dad, brother and sister along with their spouses.

"Dang girl—"

"Don't start," I interrupt my brother Cameron when we get to the table. "Your mom is enough."

"So, what happened to Jeff?" Taylor asks before I can sit down good.

"You know what happened, he broke things off."

My mother sighs, loud.

"What was that for?" I ask her.

"You're not getting any younger Chance. When are you going to settle down?"

"When the right one comes along." I tensely say.

"Well, you sure in hell will not find him spending years in dead end relationships," she scolds. "Look at your brother and sister, they've settled down and enjoying married life."

"I am well aware of that mother but like I've told you before, I am not them. Now, can we please talk about something else?"

"Oh, we definitely know that," Taylor expresses. "You really should let me fix you up with one of Travis' friends when we get back home. I know just the person too. He's faithful and loving just like my man."

I roll my eyes. "No thank you."

The waiter walks up, introduces himself as Laurence and takes our drink order. As soon as he leaves, Taylor continues.

"I don't see why not, it can't be worse than your previous relationships," she drags out the s. "At the rate you're going, you'll never find anybody on your own."

"And God knows, you will not be fertile forever. You'll be forty in two days. Keep this up and your eggs will be dry and brittle by the time you find the right one," mom chimes in causing Taylor and Cameron to laugh.

I close my eyes for a split second before opening them to everybody looking at me.

"Got doggone, can there be one freaking dinner without all this. Look, I appreciate your concern, but from this minute forward please keep your suggestions to yourself. One, I didn't ask for them. Two, it's my life and three, I don't need or want the ridicule, judgement and anything else."

"Honey, nobody is judging you, this is all out of love."

"Love, yeah right," I mumble.

"Chance," mom continues, "maybe if you fixed yourself up—"

"Camilla, leave the girl alone," my dad, Arthur finally says.

"No dad let her speak. Go ahead mom and tell me what I need to do to get and keep a man like dad, Travis or Cameron since y'all have perfect men and all the answers."

"Don't get sassy with me missy. I'm not one of your little friends. Everything I've ever done has been out of wanting the best for you."

"Sure," I scoff. "Like putting me in a fat camp when I was ten even though I was averaging normal size, forcing me to cut my hair because you didn't like the texture or stopping me from singing. Is that your best for me?"

"Yes, of course you'd think differently."

I laugh and shake my head, wishing the waiter would come with my shot of tequila.

"Like I was saying," mom goes on. "You need to get rid of these spider looking things in your head, lose twenty pounds and get a new wardrobe. God knows I'm sick of looking at you like this."

Everybody at the table snickers except my dad who's shaking his head.

"Wow, with family like this who need enemies."

"You know I'm right."

I finally get my drink. I down it as Laurence stands with his pad to take orders. I ask him to give us a minute.

"No, you're not and I'm sick of it. Since we're being all honest and loving, I really don't give a flying flip what any of you all think. For far too long I've stood by and allowed you and men like Jeff to do and say whatever to me. I kept quiet to not hurt feelings while mine were

being walked over. Now though, I've changed my mind. If you can dish it then take it. Y'all have the audacity to judge me when Taylor, you think your size eight can keep a husband who hasn't been faithful for as long as you've known him, and he loves thick thighs, by the way."

"You're lying," Taylor angrily hits the table before Travis grabs her, whispering in her ear.

"Olivia, you're smiling like you got yourself a treat in my brother when all the men in our family are whores, including my dad."

They all gasp.

"Mom, the only reason I'm letting you slide is because I respect my elders yet Matthew seven and three says, and you know it already, but I'll share it anyway. *"And why do you look at the speck in your brother's eye, but do not consider the plank in your own eye?"* Next time think before y'all come for me because I ain't the same chick who boarded the plane in

Memphis," I tell them putting my napkin on the table and getting up. "Have a great night."

Chapter 6

I go upstairs to my room. Slumping down on the bed, I fall back.

"Lord, forgive me. I need you to guide me and cover my mouth for the remaining of these days. I don't know why my family treats me like they do, but I will no longer sit by and be disrespected, neither will I figure it out. I love them like your word says but I don't have to like them. I'm trying to give grace," I say wiping the tears. "I'm trying God, but I need your help. Tell me what you'd have me to do in relation to my life and relationship. I know I've made a lot of mistakes, now I'm taking my hand off and waiting until you send my husband. Oh, can you make sure his heart is in you, he's sexy with all his teeth, financially and mentally stable and loves to laugh. Please and amen."

I check to see what time the swimming pool closes before putting on a swimming suit and cover, grabbing the bag with my kindle, phone, headphones and a towel; deciding to spend some quiet time by the pool under the moonlight. After a few laps and getting caught up on the book, *FYI I Cheat Back by BM Hardin*, I look at the time on my phone and see it is after eleven. I pack up my things and begin to head inside.

When I get to the door, I realize I don't have my key.

"Crap," I mumble right before I hear laughing coming from around the corner. I walk over to the gazebo.

"Excuse me, can one of you let me in the door, I left my key."

When the girl moves from the lap of the man, his eyes widen.

"Chance what are you doing here?" he asks standing up to fix his shorts.

"Um," I say looking around, "it's a public pool Travis."

"Uh, I, uh; it's not what it looks like." He stutters.

"Dude, I really don't give a crap what it looks like. Can you let me in or not?"

"Uh yea, let me get my stuff."

When he moves, I look over at ole girl whose face looks familiar.

"Do I know you from somewhere?" I ask her.

Travis looks at her, his eyes giving off the keep your mouth closed message.

"Wait, you're his assistant. Wow, okay," I laugh. "I bet Taylor doesn't know this, does she Mr. Loving and Faithful?"

"Look Chance, can you please not say anything to your sister? Please," he begs.

"And break up a happy home, I wouldn't dare. Now will you let me in the freaking door?"

He grabs his wallet and towel from the seat and we walk towards the door. He opens it for me and when I walk in, he walks in behind me, the chick going in a different direction.

"So, do you always bring your assistant on vacation?"

"It's not like that."

"Okay, sure but you don't have to end your night on my behalf," I say as I press the button.

When it opens, Taylor is standing there with her swimsuit on.

"Chance, Travis, what are y'all doing?" she questions looking from me to him.

"What does it look like? We're getting on the elevator stupid." I reply, moving around her.

She puts her hand up to stop me and I slap it away. "Where are you two coming from?" She looks at Travis. "Why are you with her?"

The elevator is chiming by now.

"My name is Chance and not her. Now move because I'm tired and not in the mood to argue with you."

"I'm not moving until one of you tell me where y'all are coming from." She says pushing me back to let the doors close.

I slap her hand away again. "Keep your hands off of me Taylor." I press the up button and the doors open.

"Travis baby, you can tell me. Was she trying to sleep with you?"

"Tay—"

I cut him off, stopping and turning back to her. "First of all, trick, I wouldn't touch a biscuit you've touched let alone a man. Secondly, I don't need to try and sleep with anybody because boo, thick thighs are like oxygen, they save lives. Isn't that right Travis?"

"You've always been jealous and after the dinner fiasco you probably want to get back at me, don't you? Admit it, you want the life I got. I see the way you look at him. You can't find a faithful man of your own, so you'll try to get mine."

I laugh. "Girl, there's nothing you got that I want, and I would be offended, but seeing you don't have a faithful man either, I'll let it slide." I wink at Travis whose caramel complexion is turning red.

"What is that supposed to mean?" she asks as the elevator opens and I step on. "What does that mean?" she yells again.

I throw the deuces as the doors close with her screaming my name.

The next morning, I get up early because I'm starving. I shower and out on a maxi dress and flats. I fix my locs to fit under a fedora and apply some mascara, eyeliner and lip gloss. Once I'm done, I grab my bag and head downstairs. Making it to the restaurant, I'm greeted by the hostess.

"Good morning ma'am, will anyone else be joining you?"

"No, it's just me."

"No problem, please follow me."

She leads me to a table near the back that has an amazing view of the ocean.

"Is this okay?" she asks.

"This is great."

"Juan is your server and he'll be right over."

I'm looking over the menu when Juan comes to take my drink order. I ask for a pineapple mimosa while I decide on breakfast.

"Chance?"

I look up to see Mason.

"Hey," I say getting up to give him a hug. "Would you care to join me?"

"I'd love too," he says turning to the hostess.

Once he is seated Juan comes back with my drink. He takes Mason's drink order and walks off.

"I thought you were meeting your family."

"Oh, they're here."

He laughs at the way I say it. "That bad?"

"Worse," I express sipping my drink. "They're staying on a different floor, thank God and let's just say, dinner didn't go well last night."

Juan comes back, and we place our food order as my phone vibrates with a call from my mom. I look at it, show it to him and press decline.

"Do you need to get that?"

"Nope," I say turning it off and placing it in my bag.

We talk while waiting on our food. I tell him I'm 39 with no children, I work as a business analyst for a big company in Memphis and I used to be a worship leader. I admit putting singing on the back burner because Jeff said it was overshadowing him. I also share a little about my family drama, although I don't go into detail. I didn't want to scare him off.

I find out he's 40, with a 19-year-old daughter and has been a pastor for ten years. Ministry is his full-time job and he is very passionate about it. He and his late wife met in middle school and nine months ago she died from a rare cancer that claimed her life four months after the diagnosis.

"Why are you looking at me like that?" he asks after Juan sits our food down.

"I'm sorry, I didn't mean to stare but talking to you is so easy. It feels like I've known you a lot longer than a few hours."

"I got it like that," he smirks popping the collar on his shirt.

"Oh really," I laugh.

He shakes his head, holding out his hand to me to say grace.

When he's done, he lays his fork down. "Chance, I must admit you've been a fresh wind for me. I was dreading this trip because I'd be alone but meeting you has been, um," he stops, and I look at him confused. "It's, I don't know how to say this."

"I'm a big girl Mason just say it."

"Meeting you on the plane threw me for a loop. Not in a bad way," he corrects, "but I was taken aback by your name."

"Why?"

"This may sound weird, but three nights ago God woke me from my sleep with the word chance ringing loudly in my ear. I got up and He led me to Ecclesiastes nine and eleven."

"The race isn't given to the swift?" I ask baffled.

"There's so much more to that verse." He pulls his phone from his pocket. "Solomon says, "*I have observed something else under the sun. The fastest runner doesn't always win the race, and the strongest warrior doesn't always win the battle. The wise sometimes go hungry, and the skillful are not necessarily wealthy. And those who are educated don't always lead successful lives. It is all decided by chance, by being in the right place at the right time.*""

Chapter 7

"Wow, I don't think I've ever read that verse in its entirety."

"Solomon wondered why isn't the race given to the swift or the battle to the strong when that's logically who'd be the people to win. Yet God says, sometimes time and chance happens that causes things not to work like we expect them too. Time and chance both have a way of changing our plans and it's not always a bad thing. For me, I didn't think it would be possible to enjoy this trip alone, but time and chance happened for two newly single people to meet. And if possible, I won't have to be alone."

"What is that supposed to mean? You think because I was dumped and on vacation by myself, I'm desperate. Is this the only reason you're here?"

"No, please calm down. I didn't mean to upset you," he sighs. "I apologize if my words insinuated anything other than wanting to enjoy this vacation with you. Maybe a dinner or walk, that's it. I never considered you to be desperate."

I wipe a tear that slips from my eye.

"I didn't mean for my poetic justice moment to make you cry. It seems that's all I've done since we've met."

"I think it's best I go," I tell him.

"No Chance, please don't. Tell me what you're thinking."

"Mason, I've been through my fair share of relationships and I'm not saying this is what's happening here, but I'm tired. Tired of giving myself to people who don't have the skills to handle the heart, personality, worth and glory of a strong black woman. I'm 39 years old, unmarried, no children and the product of a family who knit picks every facet of my life

from my weight to the men I date. They don't seem to understand how hurtful—I'm sorry. I didn't mean for breakfast to be a therapy session."

"No, please go on."

I exhale. "I believed in the last man who said he loved me, the one before that and the one before that. Yet, all my family see is the number of relationships and blame me, never understanding that I'm the one left with the broken heart, tears and sleepless nights. They want me to settle down with a good man, hell, I want that too. And while I believe in chances, I love the concept of love and I pray to one day receive the love I'm meant to have, I don't know if it's even possible anymore."

"With God all things are possible."

I turn my head to him and glare. "Really?"

"I don't mean that to sound as cliché as it does, but it's true. Chance," he takes my hand, "I don't want you to think I'm here because I feel sorry for you and vice versa. I shared what God told me even though I don't know what it means for either of us. Maybe I needed to be there for you or you needed to be here for me. Nonetheless, I'm happy to have been in the right place to meet you."

"Phew. This breakfast turned into more than I'd planned, yet it's what I needed. Thank you."

"Would you take a walk with me after we eat our cold food?" he laughs. "There is a great little coffee shop not far from here that I found yesterday."

"I'd love too."

We finish our food and head out. Getting to the door, he holds it open before placing his hand on the small of my back, allowing me to go in front of him. Outside, he does it again as we're walking pass a crowd of people. I look at him and he quickly retracts it.

"I apologize," he says.

"No, please don't. I didn't look at you because I was uncomfortable. This may sound weird, but that simple gesture makes me feel safe. Is it crazy to be this old and never to have felt that?"

"Not at all and I apologize for not asking you first, but I do it out of instinct. A man should always make you feel safe in his presence. When we're walking pass a crowd, I'm supposed to protect you and I do that by placing my hand there. As the head, it's also the responsibility of the man to guide. This can be accomplished by placing my hand there, ensuring we're both going in the same direction."

"To be forty, you have an old soul." I reply.

"I was raised by my grandfather who instilled old wisdom into me," he smiles. "He and my grandmother were married for sixty-two years."

"It shows and I'm grateful."

We spend the next three hours sightseeing around the resort. I tell him a little more about my family, seeing Travis last night and Taylor's reaction.

"Wow," he says. "You have yourself a full-on Brady Bunch, huh?"

"More like Flowers in the Addict," I chuckle. "Take my advice, if ever you should be in their vicinity, brace yourself."

"Making a mental note."

We are laughing when we make it back to the hotel. While walking to the elevator, I turn my phone back on to exchange numbers for dinner tonight. When the doors open, we come face to face with Taylor and my mom.

"Well, if it isn't the family whoremonger," Taylor mocks.

I roll my eyes, ignoring her.

"Mason, thank you for spending your morning with me."

"My pleasure," he kisses my cheek.

"I know you aren't going to act like we're not standing here," Mom jeers. "Hello sir, my name is

Camilla McGhee, Chance's mother and this is her sister Taylor."

"Hi, it's nice to meet the two of you."

Taylor looks him up and down. "You're just becoming the all-around resort slut, huh? Get your husbands ladies because there's a homewrecker on the prowl." She says loud enough for people to stop and stare.

I just look at her. "Did that make you feel better, looking like Peppa Pig with this pink—girl is this velvet? You're going to burn up."

"Both of y'all stop it. You're causing a scene," mom looks around. "Chance, tell me you aren't messing with this girl's husband."

I turn my head to look at her sideways because obviously she's been drinking pond water. "Do you actually think I'm desperate and dry enough to sleep with Travis, mother?"

"Well what were you doing with him last night?"

"He let me in the freaking door," I exclaim before Mason touches my arm.

"Let's take some different elevators," he offers.

"Don't walk away from me," mom snatches my arm causing Mason to move in front of me.

"Sir, this is family business and I'm talking to my daughter."

"You can talk to her, but not like this. Let her go."

"Where's is your wife," Taylor snares, "because I'm sure you have one?"

"Ma'am, your concern should be with your husband and not my affairs." Mason states. "Please excuse us."

We prepare to leave again, but mom stops me. "I was giving you the benefit of the doubt, thinking you had better morals than to go after your sister's husband but apparently I was wrong. You should be ashamed of yourself."

I let out a long breath of air. "You know what, I am ashamed."

"See I told you she was a whore." Taylor adds.

By this time, more people are staring.

"I am ashamed to have been born into this family." I turn to Mason. "I am sorry you've had to witness this foolishness. Thank you for this morning but I will need to take a raincheck on dinner, I'm going home."

"Yeah, do like you always do, run fatty." Taylor quips.

I lunge at her, but Mason grabs me.

"You know I used to feel sorry for you but now I know why your husband cheats. You are a disgusting human being and if I never see you again, it'll be too soon. Mom, I hope you and daddy enjoy the rest of your vacation or don't, I can care less either way."

I stop. "Oh Taylor, while you're so busy trying to convince everybody of my affair with your husband, he's probably off banging his assistant who he brought on the "family" vacation."

Chapter 8

"Ugh, I'm sorry you had to experience that. I can assure you, I'm not petty like this all the time."

"No, don't do that. They should be the ones apologizing to you. I've never seen so much contempt in the eyes of a mother and sister."

"The saddest part, I've never understood why they treat me this way. Sure, my skin color is darker and I'm heavier, but I don't deserve this from them or anybody."

"I agree," he takes my hands. "You're beautiful and if they can't see that, there's nothing you can possibly do or say to make them. What you have to do is stop apologizing and explaining who you are. Stand boldly as the woman God made you."

"Thank you and you're right."

"Are you really leaving?"

"Heck no. I'm not about to let them ruin my vacation. I'm sick of them and no longer giving them control over how I react to their pettiness. I've always been the one to make amends when I haven't done anything wrong. That's over."

The elevator stops on my floor.

"May I walk you to your room?"

"Please."

Getting to my door, I put the key in and he holds it open.

"Will I see you for dinner?"

"You will," I smile, "and thank you for standing up for me. It means a lot."

"Chance," I hear my dad's voice.

"Ugh, it's my dad." I introduce them and Mason kisses me on the cheek and walks away.

"What's up dad?" I ask as he follows me inside.

"We missed you for breakfast this morning."

"Nobody missed me, so please don't act like you did," I sternly say. "Look daddy, I love you but I'm tired of being mistreated by this family. For as long as I can remember I'm always the one being talked about and judged. I used to wonder why, but I'm no longer going to spend my good energy figuring it out. None of you have ever stood up for me. I was embarrassed downstairs by Taylor yelling and calling me a slut while mom looked on because she actually thinks I'd sleep with Travis. Do you know how humiliating that is?"

He sighs. "That's just the way they are Button."

"No, this is what has been accepted because you let mom dictate everything. Due to that, she's allowed Taylor and Cameron to follow in her footsteps. What about me? You see the way they treat me, and you never say anything."

"That's not true. I got on your mom and the rest of them last night after you left. I don't like the way they treat you Button."

"Stop calling me that," I say louder than I meant. "If you cared about how they treat me, you would have done or said something long before now. From this point on, I'm done being the brunt of their jokes. For the next four days, act like I'm not here. If you see me, don't even bother speaking and I'll return the favor." I walk over and open the door. "I mean it daddy. If you can't stand up for me in public, don't do it in private. Goodbye."

I shut the door behind him, not giving him a chance to say anything else. I take my Bible from the nightstand, walking out to the balcony. I lay it in the chair before looking up to the sky.

"God, heal my brokenness so it doesn't stand in the way of my happiness. Restore what harsh words and criticism has torn away from my spirit. Forgive me for any sin or iniquity that keeps me out of your will. Strengthen me with what I need to endure the battles of flesh. Give me peace, but most of all, give me understanding. I may not know why things are like they are and I'm okay with that. Guard my heart, mind, ears, eyes and spirit. Thank you for giving me another chance and I pray to not mess it up, this time. What is for me, don't let me block it and what's not for me, you shield me from it. This I pray, amen."

I spend a little more time reading Ecclesiastes nine from the conversation with Mason during breakfast. Although I don't know what God is doing through my encounter with Mason, I'm grateful for another chance at life and when the time is right, love.

6:47 PM

I'm standing in the full-length mirror looking at myself. I have thirteen minutes before I'm supposed to meet Mason for dinner. I'm nervous and excited.

"Get it together Chance. It's just dinner." I run my hand over the peach colored top and white jeans. I slip into colorful heels, ensure my lip gloss is good before turning off the lights.

Opening the door, Mason startles me.

"Oh my God," I say clasping my hand over my chest. "You scared me."

"I apologize," he smiles. "I was getting ready to knock when the door opened. You look beautiful, by the way."

"Thank you."

"Shall we?"

Getting to the lobby, I get ready to head towards the restaurant, when he places his hand on the small of my back.

"This way."

He leads me out to a waiting Rolls Royce.

"Fancy," I smile getting inside.

For the next thirty minutes, we ride in silence. Pulling up to a harbor, the driver opens the door to help me out.

"Wow, this is breathtaking," I tell him stepping onto the boat.

"Good afternoon sir and ma'am, my name is Captain Federico Ajani and my staff, and I are here to ensure you have an enjoyable night. Please make yourselves comfortable as we'll be setting sail in ten minutes and dinner will be served promptly at 8:15."

"You did all of this for me?"

"Actually, it was free, and I couldn't pass it up. I'm kidding," he chuckles. "I wanted tonight to be free from drama, so to keep you from running into your family, why not get out and enjoy the night. Also consider it an early birthday gift. You only turn 40 once."

I stand there for a few seconds.

"I hope—"

I throw my arms around him before he can finish the sentence. "Thank you."

"Dinner was amazing," I express walking to the main deck with Mason. He goes over to a speaker and when the music begins, I look at him.

"What do you know about The Staple Singers?"

"Let me take you there," he sings holding out his hand to me.

I dance over to him joining in. "I know a place," we both say.

"Ain't nobody worried. Ain't no smiling faces." I continue singing and he pulls me to him.

We continue to dance together until it changes to Too Much by Luther Vandross.

"Okay Pastor Gray," I joke turning to face him.

"I still got a little funk in me," he laughs.

For the next few hours, I enjoy every minute of the night. By the time we make it back to the hotel, I didn't want to part ways with him.

"Thank you," he says standing outside my door.

"You're thanking me after all you've done tonight. Why?"

"For not being afraid to be yourself in front of me."

"You make it easy and while we're giving out accolades, thank you for an amazing evening. I can't tell you the last time I've had this much fun."

I lean in to kiss him on the cheek and instead our lips touch, he deepens it.

"Find your voice again Chance," he says kissing me one last time and I look at him knowing exactly what he means. "Sweet dreams and happy early birthday."

"Thank you," I blush.

Chapter 9

Getting inside the room, I drop my clutch on the table and kick off my shoes before falling onto the bed.

"Lord, I don't know what you're doing but heal my heart."

After a few minutes, I get my phone to upload pictures from the boat.

Once it powers on, I open Facebook to over 99+ notifications. I click one and my mouth drops.

This worship leader can rock my mic any night

I don't even have to look through the pictures to know what they are. They're ones Jeff took of me when we first got together. Pictures he promised he'd deleted. I was stupid for even allowing him to take them.

"Oh my God," I mumble as tears spill from my eyes.

I scroll through a few of the posts, stopping at one from Wednesday, a fellow worship leader.

We all know who's responsible for leaking those photos. Pastor Jeffrey Walker, if I should even call you that. You and your flunkies should be ashamed of yourself. You'd willingly embarrass a woman who spent the last three years by your side being for you what you couldn't even fathom being for her. I pray the vengeance of God reigns down on you and your fleshly followers as quickly as these went viral. By the way, she's gorgeous! #dirtydog #workeroftheenemy

I dial her number.

"Chance, I'm so sorry. I tried to call you."

"My phone was off. Sis, I knew he would hit below the belt, but not like this," I tell her. "It was embarrassing enough that he dumped me and now this. This is humiliating Wednesday."

"I know doll, but me and your fellow worship leaders have your back."

"I saw your post. Thank you."

"You don't have to thank me, that's what friends are for."

"I'm so disgusted and disappointed with him."

"He's only mad things aren't working out like he'd hoped. The congregation at St. Joseph is getting smaller by the Sunday. Truth be told, we knew it was you helping him with his sermons. That Negro ain't talked about nothing substantial and filling since you left."

I chuckle.

"You're going to be okay Chance. If it's any consolation, you are absolutely stunning in those photos."

"Thanks, I guess."

"You are. Don't allow this to ruin your vacation and your birthday. Let things run their course."

"What other choice do I have?" I exhale. "I'll talk to you later."

I see the text and voicemail messages from Jeff. I delete them all without reading or listening before throwing the phone on the bed and getting up. Walking around the room, I feel myself getting angry.

"God, why? Why?" I yell. "What else do I have to suffer through? My family, my relationship and now my dignity. What more?" I collapse into the floor. "What more God?"

A knock on the door.

"Chance," I hear Mason call out.

I don't acknowledge him.

"I'm here when you need me," he says. "Room 922."

For the next few hours, I sit on the floor still dressed from dinner. My phone has been vibrating constantly and the room phone has been ringing. I'm gazing ahead at the wall trying to figure out when things turned for the worse in my life. Where did I take a wrong turn? I used to sing for the Lord, I read my Bible, I pray, I

repent, I love people who don't seem to love me, I forgive, I work and don't steal, I pay tithes and sow seeds. Yet, here's where I find myself with images of my half naked body being circulated around the internet.

"What do I do God?" I question out loud.

The next morning I'm sitting on the beach, attached to the hotel, watching the sunrise. I've been silently praying to God. Then I hear …

Find your voice again Chance.

I open my mouth while the tears flow and the first song that comes to mind is Something Has to Break by Kierra Sheard.

"Tear down every lie, set the wrong thing right cause when you have your way, something has to break. Something has to break. Right now, in your name something has to break. Oh God," I say raising my hand to the sky. "Something has to break. I believe you'll lead me through it, I believe you'll get me to it and

I believe that you will do it right now. Please God, something has to break."

I begin to hum and speak in tongue.

"Something has to break," I repeat over and over moving to my knees and stretching out my arms. "I'm sorry God, I've messed up. Break away anything that's not meant and destroy what I don't have the strength to do. Break it right now God, I plead in the name of Jesus. I've tried this thing for too long on my own, I can't do it anymore. I kept quiet when you told me to sing. I put people and things before you. I'm sorry Father. Hear my heart's cry and heal me. Even if you have to break me, do it. More of you and less of me," I pray beginning to sing again. "Something has to break. I believe you'll lead me through it. I believe you'll get me to it. I believe that you will do it right now."

I wrap my arms around myself calling on the name of Jesus.

My eyes open when I hear a guitar and I notice a few people have stopped and joined in on my worship. I didn't realize I was singing loud enough for them to hear. I gaze out and become awed by the move of God. After a few minutes, I look at the gentleman who's playing, he nods, and I lift my hand to him. He quiets the music as I belt, "I need thee oh, I need thee. Every hour, I need thee. Oh, bless me now my savior, I come to thee." I repeat it a few times before praying again. When I stop, he continues as more people trickle over.

We spend the next thirty minutes in unusual worship. It's something I've never experienced before. Afterwards, a young lady walks over to ask my name. I give it to her before introducing myself to the young man playing the guitar. He tells me his name is Raphael.

"That was amazing," he beams. "I've never felt the presence of God so heavily like this before. Crazy thing, I was getting ready to give up on playing music because I thought I'd lost my love for it. Then I came across you and at first, I could only see your lips moving. But then, you opened your mouth and wow. I'm getting chills thinking about it. Ms. Chance God is real," he chokes up. "I asked Him for a sign and I walk out on the beach, expecting to be alone and there you were. I interrupted your alone time with God and now, I'm standing here taking up your time."

"It's no problem, I'm glad you did actually. This morning was the first time I've sung in a while and I guess we both needed the reminder of how real God is."

"Amen. It was nice to meet you Chance."

"You too."

Chapter 10

I walk back inside the hotel and to my room. After showering, I lay down for a much-needed nap. The sound of knocking wakes me.

"Housekeeping," she calls out before the door opens. "Oh, my apologies ma'am, I thought the room was empty."

I sit up. "It's fine, I forgot to put the sign on the door. However, don't worry about cleaning but I'd like some fresh towels."

"No problem."

I get up and get some money from my purse for a tip. Once she leaves, I wash my face and get dressed. Staring at my reflection in the mirror, I smile. "Happy Birthday Chance Alondra McGhee. May you find the happiness you deserve. May you walk into the fullness of God's call on your life. May you never lose your voice again and may this be the beginning of the best years of your life."

Realizing it's after one, I decide to get something to eat from the resort's restaurant before taking a walk. Making it downstairs, I notice a few people pointing at me. I instantly cringe.

"Good afternoon, you're Ms. Chance, right?" a gentleman stops me at the door.

"Yes, but—"

He clasps his hands together in the prayer posture, nods and walks off before I can ask him how he knows that. I stand there as another man does the same thing then a group of women smile and nod.

I turn around in a circle, starting to feel dizzy.

"Chance," Mason says. "Are you okay? Chance, hey."

"No," I admit. "Why is everybody staring? Did they see the pictures? God. I need to get out of here." I start to panic.

"Wait, please calm down."

"No Mason, I need some air."

"Chance, this isn't about your pictures," he states following me outside and grabbing me by the arm. "Look at me." He takes my face into his hands. "Chance, look at me."

I open my eyes.

"Did you see them?" I ask as tears fall.

"Do you not recognize the amazing gift you are?"

"I don't feel like a gift right now. I feel like I've been gutted and thrown out like trash. Mason, my entire being is hurt. After last night with you, I thought things were turning around and now," I wipe the tears, "I don't know."

I turn to walk away until I hear my voice singing.

"Oh my God, someone recorded that?"

"A young lady who works in housekeeping was on the beach this morning. She posted it on the hotel's

Facebook page and it's been shared a few thousand times since."

My hand is over my mouth, in shock.

"You found your voice," he says.

"I—I, it was only worship."

"It was more than that. Bible says in Genesis fifty and twenty, *"You intended to harm me, but God intended it all for good. He brought me to this position, so I could save the lives of many people."* It may have been worship for you, but it was a witness of God's power for those watching."

I'm shaking my head no. "I don't, I don't even know what to say." I tell him as I continue to cry. "My mouth and heart desire to worship God but I feel so dirty. This morning was my private time with Him and I don't know if I'll ever be able to sing in front of people again. Jeff took that from me."

"Don't give him the power too. Chance, people will look at you whether you're doing good or bad. Yet, this

gift God has given you shouldn't be silenced. Your voice is needed."

"I hear you but—" my stomach growls. "I haven't eaten today," I tell him.

"I'm going to take that as God's sign to there being no buts. Your gift will make room for you and I don't find it coincidental that all of this is happening on your 40th birthday."

"Why?"

"It was forty years when God delivered the children of Israel from the wilderness. Chance, I believe God is releasing you from yours. Just like He asked them in Deuteronomy eight and two, *"Remember how the Lord your God led you through the wilderness for these forty years, humbling you and testing you to prove your character, and to find out whether or not you would obey his commands?"* Now, it's time for you to walk according to God's will for your life."

"Are you always in pastoral role?" I chuckle.

"Only every day and twice on Sunday. Now, may I take you to lunch?"

"You may."

After spending a few hours with Mason, I walk into my room singing and smiling. I begin to undress for a shower. The resort is having a show on the beach tonight and I'm planning to attend as a birthday gift to myself.

I continue dancing until there's a knock on the door. I put my dress back on and open it.

"Good afternoon ma'am, this is for you." The gentleman says handing me a card.

He turns to walk off before I can respond. Closing the door, I open the envelope.

"Happy birthday. It's only right to celebrate in one of the prettiest places with dinner and a moonlight dance. I'd be honored if you'd do me the pleasure of giving me another Chance."

I giggle like a school girl as I finish reading the card.

Later on, I take my time getting ready for tonight. I style my locs in a knot on the top of my head with pieces hanging down. My makeup is always simple with mascara, eyeliner and lip gloss. I get dressed in a pair of burgundy sequin pants, white off the shoulder dressy top and heels. I packed this in case my family acted right for my birthday and decided to do dinner. Now, it won't go to waste.

I finish in the bathroom, grab a jacket, the note and my clutch purse.

Following the directions, I head to the room designated. Opening the door, I walk further in and gasp when I see the room is decorated in burgundy and white, my favorite colors.

"Oh my God," I say walking further in. "Hello," I call out.

"Happy Birthday beautiful."

"Aw hell. Jeff what are you doing here?"

"I came to surprise you for your birthday."

"A surprise would have been a brand new, burgundy 2021 Range Rover with twelve miles. You, you're anything but a surprise. Goodbye."

He runs in front of me. "Babe, I know you're upset, and you have every right to be. I was wrong for everything."

"Oh gee, thank you Jeff. You just made me the happiest woman in the world. Negro please. Your half ass apology means nothing to me anymore. You humiliated me and for what? I didn't do anything to you. Yet, had I posted pictures of your little toy soldier, how would you have felt."

"You're right and I apologize but Chance I did all of this for you."

"And? You could have gotten up on stilts and drew stars on the ceiling with a crayon and I still wouldn't take you back. Goodnight Jeff."

"Girl suck it up and take this man back," Taylor says coming in from a side door. It's not like you have any other options."

"Maybe I don't, but if I needed a man to save my very existence on this earth and he was the last one, I'd rather die. And who asked you anyway, Penny Proud of the Proud Family? Don't you have a husband you need to watch?"

A door opens and my mom, dad and the rest of the family comes in followed by Mason.

"Mason, what are you doing here?"

"I asked him to come. Seeing y'all were so chummy," Taylor smirks.

I turn back, and Jeff is down on one knee.

"Fool, please get up."

"Chance don't throw away three years of our life together. Please forgive me, give me another chance and I promise to make up for everything."

I start to laugh. "This has got to be a joke. Mason, do you have any holy oil because it's clear I need an exorcist because either I'm possessed, or they are."

Jeff gets up and walks closer to me.

"Baby give me a chance to explain."

I flinch when he goes to touch me, so he steps back. "Explain?" I chuckle. "No thanks. I don't need you to explain anything to me. You've embarrassed me enough in this lifetime and the next. You better be glad I'm being this nice and for your sake, it's best you leave me alone. Now, for the last time, goodbye." I walk over to Mason. "Would you care to join me for dinner tonight?"

He smiles. "I'd love too."

"I told y'all this wouldn't work," I hear Jeff say.

Chapter 11

I slowly turn around. "Do what?"

Taylor is smiling while sipping a glass of champagne.

"Look," Jeff exhales, "I didn't want to come here, but I'm desperate. I'm on thin ice with the deacons of St. Joseph and—"

"And you thought coming here, setting this up was going to do what exactly? Negro, I'd rather do fifteen years in a Jamaican prison than to marry you. You don't deserve me."

He puffs up. "Look, it's not like you have a lot of choices Chance, come on. Besides, your mother says you need me to remove your shame and she promised if I came here and did all this, you'd take me back."

"Dude—" Mason steps forward but I stop him.

"My shame, are we back in Nazareth? First off Pooh, I have nothing to be ashamed of because I'm not the one putting people to sleep in worship. Second, my mother is the last person you should be listening too. She's never liked me nor had my best interest at heart. You'd be better off asking my kindergarten teacher."

"That's not true," she says. "I don't like your ways sometimes. You remind me so much of—"

"Camilla," my dad says pulling her arm. "Don't."

"I remind you of who?" I ask.

"Rose."

"Grandma Rose? What does she have to do with this?"

"That woman never liked me, and she made my life a living hell from the moment Arthur took me to her house. She'd picked apart everything about me from my hair to my clothes."

"The same way you do me."

"You look just like her," she screams. "Every time I look at you, I see that witch. From the dark complexion, to the curly hair and even the way you walk and smile. Hell, you even sing like her," she shivers. "All the hell I had to endure at the hands of that lady then my first child comes out looking like her. You talk about a slap in the face."

"That's enough," my dad belts.

"Wait," I laugh, "all these years you've treated me like I was the spawn of Satan because of my grandmother, a lady I never even got the chance to meet? Please tell me you're joking."

"Does it look like it? You're the spitting image of her and I cringe thinking about her. Come to think of it, it's the reason you can't keep a relationship," she huffs. "Everybody knew Rose was a round the way girl. Thank God her genes skipped my other two babies. Having one constant reminder of her was enough."

"Mane, I knew this family was the epitome of dysfunction, but this takes things to an entirely different level. You hate me because I look like my grandmother. Mother, you need help."

"I'm not crazy," she declares.

"Oh yeah sis, you're definitely ranking up there. For as long as I can remember, you've projected your anger for a lady whose been dead thirty-nine years on your oldest daughter. You always made difference in me when it came to clothes, toys and even your affection. If you didn't love or want me, you should have put me up for adoption."

"Your father wouldn't let me," she states matter-of-factly.

"Camilla, that's enough." Dad screams.

"No, don't stop her when you've never tried before. I only hate you talked her out of it because being in the foster system had to be better than growing up in the house with y'all." I look at each of them. "It's bad enough my own mother hates me for something I had no control over, but to know you all have allowed it to consume your love for me, disgusts me." I tell Taylor and Cameron.

"Chance, I'm sorry," Cameron says walking towards me. "You're right. I have allowed the way mom treats you to taint our relationship and I'm sorry. Please forgive me. I didn't know."

"You're forgiven and forgotten. I never want anything else to do with any of you."

"Wait," Jeff says. "Since we're confessing things," he waves his hand, "I may as well come clean too."

"Jeff, what are you doing?" Taylor questions jumping in front of him. "Don't do this," she pleads.

He smiles, stepping around her. "Taylor and I have been seeing each other for the last year."

"He's lying," she cries looking at Travis.

"Yeah, I'm lying about that but," he cuts his eyes at her, "I wasn't the one who posted your pictures to Facebook. It was Taylor."

"Lord, you've got to help me." I say taking a deep breath as my hands form into fists. "Lord, please."

"Chance, let's go." Mason tells me.

"How would Taylor get my pictures Jeff? You're the only one who had them and you lied like they were deleted."

"They were in my iCloud account."

"And?"

"She called asking for pictures of you saying she was putting something together for your birthday. I was in the middle of something and gave her my iCloud information. She must have saw the photos and posted them from a fake Facebook page."

"Why should I believe you? You're a lying, despicable shell of a man who has hurt me almost as much as them. I know Taylor can do some conniving stuff, but that's low even for her."

He shrugs getting his phone, handing it to me. I begin to read the thread of text messages.

Jeff: Taylor, I know it was you who leaked Chance's photos.

Taylor: I don't know what you're talking about.

Jeff: Stop lying. Those photos were in my iCloud and it's no coincidence they're posted right after I give you access.

Taylor: Oops <laughing emoji> It's not like you care anyway. You dumped her, remember.

Jeff: It's still wrong and she's going to think I did it.

Taylor: Your problem.

Jeff: Not if I show her this text thread.

Taylor: Is that supposed to scare me? Tell her and I'll let it slip that you've been seeing Travis' sister behind her back for a year.

I swipe the tears from my face.

"Travis' sister huh?"

"I meant to erase that."

I throw the phone and it hits him in the mouth.

"Chance," Mason stands in front of me. "Breathe."

"Move Mason," I state my body starting to shake from anger.

"Let me take you away from here. We can go anywhere you want to celebrate your birthday."

"My own sister," I cry. "My baby sister is the one who humiliated me and now I'm going to beat her ass."

"Girl you won't touch me," she boldly says still sipping champagne. "I did what I did because you shouldn't have gone after my husband."

I push pass Mason and over to her with my mom screaming my name. I punch her so fast she doesn't have time to react.

"After all I've done for you," I scream, "and you do this to me. I was there when at seventeen you had to get an abortion and didn't want to tell your precious mother. I was the one who had to whoop Chris, your college boyfriend because he wouldn't keep his hands to himself. I was the one who bailed you out of jail when you got that DUI a few years back and I never parted my lips to tell anybody. Yet, you do this to me."

Dad grabs my arm, but I snatch away.

"Button don't do this. This isn't you."

"How do you know?" I yell at him. "How do you know who I am? Our relationship is strained because of what you allow when I never asked for any of this. You're my father. You're supposed to love and protect me. Why keep me when you knew you didn't have the balls to stand up to Camilla?"

He has tears streaming. "You're right and I'm sorry. I love you."

"This isn't love and I'm sick of pretending like it is. Y'all can have this dysfunctional ass family. After this, consider me dead."

"I'm sorry," Travis says to me. "As for you," he turns to Taylor, "we're done."

He walks out, and she gets out of mom's grip to chase him.

"Chance, please," I hear my father say to my back as the doors close behind me.

Chapter 12

It's three in the morning and I'm sitting on the balcony because I couldn't sleep. I wrap the blanket around me as I allow the tears to fall.

"Heal my heart, God. Please God, heal me." I begin to speak in tongue. "You didn't cause the hurt but it's only you who can heal. Father, I need you. Please have mercy on me and remove this anger. Father, I have no more fight in me. Hmmm," I hum. "I repent for my sins and for turning my back on you and shutting my mouth. God, give me a song and I vow to sing for you. No more will I water down your gospel. No more will I put my life in the hands of someone you didn't ordain to hold me. Protect my heart God with a password only you know that he'll have to get from you. Have mercy oh God."

I speak in tongue before I begin to sing Hear My Prayer by Callie Day.

"O Lord, please hear my prayer in the morning when I rise. It's your servant bound for glory. O dear Lord, please hear my prayer. When my work on earth is done and you come to take me home. Just to know that I am bound for glory and to hear you say, well done. Done with sin and sorrow. Have mercy. Amen."

I sit out there until the sun comes up. Once it does, I open the Facebook app and go live. It's early and I don't wait for anyone to join before I begin speaking.

"I know you all have seen the pictures of me floating around social media. They were taken three years ago by a man I thought was going to be my husband. He lied like they were deleted, but it doesn't matter now. Yesterday, I turned 40 in the beautiful Jamaica and yet it was anything but happy. However, this isn't the reason for this live because I don't need nor want pity. I'm only addressing this issue once. Yes, I was ashamed of those pictures, not anymore. You're going to get all these 190 pounds of fluffiness. Far too long I've allowed everyone else to dictate how I live. Well social media fam, today I'm taking back my power. It's been forty years and now I'm ready to walk into the fullness of who I am in God. Just in case you don't know who that is, allow me to tell you. My name is Chance Alondra McGhee and who I am is a bold, anointed, educated, strong, thick chick who's no longer taking people's shit. I've found my voice again. Oh yeah, happy Thanksgiving."

I throw the deuces, end the live, take a deep breath and prepare to live my life. After a shower, I get dressed and finish packing for my flight at one. I lay down for a quick nap because I feel a headache coming. At eleven, I get up and go downstairs. Getting off the elevator, I see Taylor with my mom and dad waiting to be seated for lunch. She has on a large pair of black shades and a big hat trying to cover the black eye I'm sure she has. Dad comes over to me.

"Are you leaving?"

"Dad, what does it look like?" I sigh.

"Button, I'm sorry about your birthday last night and now your Thanksgiving. Please stay and let's figure this out."

"Nope," I tell him.

"I'm sorry for everything and I know this is long overdue, but I pray you'll forgive me."

"Arthur," mom calls out.

"You better go before you get in trouble." I say walking up to the counter. I check out, go outside and get into the first cab headed to the airport.

❉❉❉❉❉

It's been three months since the trip to Jamaica and although Mason and I occasionally text, we haven't seen each other or actually spoken. I needed some time to get myself together and over all that happened. Dealing with all this has caused my migraines to return and there's no way I'm going back on medication because of my family. So, I've cut them off and haven't talked to my parents or siblings. My dad has called but I'm not ready to talk to him yet. I do respond to his 'love you' texts though because I do love him. As for Jeff, he married some new girl on what would have been our wedding day in February. It was all over social media although it didn't stop him from being removed from the position at St. Joseph.

Today, I've decided to visit Mason's church, Harvest Tabernacle of Praise.

"Good morning," the usher says leading me near the middle of the sanctuary as the service begins. I was thoroughly enjoying myself until the announcer asked for visitors to stand. I nervously stand and when I look up, my eyes lock with Mason who smiles. I smile back. I was asked to introduce myself and when I say my name, there are a few looks and some smiles from the congregation. I slink back down into my seat as service continues. Before altar call, the choir begins to sing, I Believe by James Fortune. It's one of my favorite songs and my soul stirs. I close my eyes and begin to sing until a young lady taps me, pointing toward the pulpit. I look at Mason who motions for me to come forward.

Reluctantly, I put my things on the chair and walk towards the front. He holds out his hand as I climb the few steps to join him.

"Will you sing for me, well for us?" he smiles.

I look at him and he mouths, please. I take a deep breath and grab the microphone. The choir sings the chorus and I take that time to close my eyes and calm my nerves because I hadn't planned on singing today. When the music changes, I lift the microphone.

"I believe the storm will soon be over. I believe the rain will go away. I believe that I can make it through it, oh I believe it's already done. I believe family will get better. I believe God will provide. I believe the promise that He made, oh I believe it's already done. I believe that my God is a healer. I believe that I will survive. I believe that God is able, oh I believe it's already done."

By the time the song is over, I'm a mess. I hand the microphone to Mason and he pulls me into a hug as the congregation claps and offers their amen and praises to God. Getting back to my seat, the young lady touches my leg and smiles. After service, people come up to shake my hand and offer hugs. By the time I make it to Mason, he has a huge smile on his face.

"I'm getting you," I say.

"Chance, I couldn't pass up the opportunity to hear that beautiful voice," he replies hugging me. "It's been a while and had it not been for texts, I'd think you were a figment of my imagination."

"I'm glad I came today. Service was awesome and much needed."

"You're more than welcome to join us," a young lady says in passing.

"What she said," he laughs. "I hope you'll stick around and join me for lunch?"

"I'd love too."

"Follow me. I have a few things to finish up and you can wait in my office. If that's okay."

"That's fine."

Inside the office, I look around at the pictures on the wall and bookcase. Mason's wife was gorgeous.

The door opens, and I turn expecting to see Mason, instead it's a female version of him.

"Hey, I'm Marcy, Pastor Gray's daughter."

"Hi, I'm Chance and it's so nice to meet you."

"What's your plan with my dad?" she blurts.

"Wow, okay, um I don't have any plans."

"Can we sit?" she asks.

"Sure."

"I apologize for being so forward. My mom passed away a year ago, today and although my dad is wise, I don't want him to jump into a relationship and be taken advantage of because he's emotional. He likes you Ms. Chance, you're all he's talked about since coming home from Jamaica, but I also know you're the first lady since my mom."

"He told me about your mom, you have my condolences. I wasn't aware what today was, however I can assure you there is no hidden agenda as it relates to me. Your dad was there for me in Jamaica and I can never repay him for that. As far as a relationship, we're not there yet. I like him too and I think only time will tell where it leads. I can tell you this, I'm not rushing."

"I can see why he likes you," she smiles. "Any other woman would have bit my head off being I'm nineteen and in my dad's business, but instead you talked to me. Thank you."

"Marcy, I have nothing to hide and I don't mind having a conversation with you because you want the best for your dad. As do I. I'd hope you'd want him to be happy."

"I do."

"Me too."

She stands and walks to the door. "Ms. Chance, my dad really does like you and if you like him, pray and let God lead you, okay?"

"I will."

When the door closes, I lean back on the couch. "Okay God, you caught me off guard with that, but I trust you." I put my air pods in and play the song I sang earlier. Once it ends, I open my eyes to replay it, but stop when I see Mason and a few other people standing in the door.

"I didn't realize you were standing there."

"I can listen to you sing all day and night," he admits waving the others off, closing the door and joining me on the couch.

"Before we go to lunch, there is something I need to talk to you about."

"Okay." I say smoothing down the front of my dress.

"I want you to be my wife."

Chapter 13

"Let me explain," he says when he notices the look on my face. "Like I shared with you before, I almost didn't take the trip to Jamaica because I thought it would be too hard to go without my wife. Then God woke me up that night and," he pauses, "I believe it was destined for our paths to cross and then you showed up today of all days."

"Your daughter told me the significance of today," I tell him.

"You met Marcy?"

"I did and you're raising a beautiful and smart daughter. She's worried about you though and who can blame her. You and your wife were together a long time."

"She's taken on the burden of trying to make sure I'm okay."

"She also said you've been talking about me." I nudge him.

"You don't understand the magnitude of our connection, do you. Chance, it's been three months and although we text, you showed up today when I needed you and you didn't even realize it. I'd been praying for God to comfort my grieving heart and He did. You're going to be my wife."

"Mason, we just met a few months ago and barely know each other. How can you be sure I'm the person for you?"

"In all fairness, you haven't given us the chance to get to know one another."

"I know but I needed time to deal with everything that happened before and during Jamaica. My life was a mess," I remark, "and I needed space to think clearly."

"How are things?"

"Well, I haven't spoken to my family since leaving there and I'm okay with that. I used to be the one to reach out, not anymore. After everything I realized I needed to protect me from the things I can control and at this point I'm going to let God deal with them."

"What about Jeff?"

"He's an entire other situation and no longer my problem. He got married on what would have been our wedding day and I'm praying for whomever she is. I guess he thought it'd salvage the relationship with St. Joseph and when it didn't, he started contacting me again."

"Do you think there's a chance you and him would get back together?"

"God no. I'll never go back to what God delivered me from. These last three months has given me the chance to rebuild a relationship with God. It was during the quiet moments I realized I was devoted to religion rather than a relationship with Him. In order to truly find

and appreciate my voice again, I had to do so by committing myself to God. I also believe it was no coincidence you'd ask me to sing that song this morning. I've had it on repeat for months. Mason, I have to believe that God will provide for me, but I don't know if rushing into a relationship is the answer."

"Chance, I'll never rush you into anything, however I'm willing to wait for you. In the meantime, can we at least get to know one another while you pray and allow God to open your heart to me?"

I chuckle. "Your daughter said something similar."

"Great minds."

"You know this is crazy, right? You're the pastor of this church. How is it going to look for you to pop up with a new girlfriend a year after your wife died?"

"Wife," he corrects. "We're way pass the girlfriend/boyfriend phase because I know what I want and that's you as my wife and hopefully the mother of my child or children."

"How can you be so sure? I'm just a forty-year-old woman you met on a plane, three months ago with a whole lot of craziness in her life. Shoot, I've spent the last three months figuring out thirty-nine years of who I used to be, and you think I'm who you want in the same time span."

"You're wrong. You're not just a woman, but you're the woman God said would give me another chance to love, honor and cherish until death do us part."

"It's only been a year though," I state. "A year Mason."

"Chance, there's a reason I asked you to sing that song this morning. It's what my wife would play during her sickness when she spent alone time with God. That song gave her hope to know and believe in God, no matter how He'd heal her. She believed it was already done and it's all I kept hearing this morning, not knowing you'd had it on repeat. I have to believe God is providing both of us another chance. Proverbs sixteen and thirty-three says, *"We may throw the dice, but the LORD determines how they fall."* Will you think about it?"

I exhale. "This is crazy but if it's God's plan for us, He'll give you the password to my heart." I smirk using his words on him.

"Indeed, he will. Now, how about that lunch?"

Three weeks later, I'm meeting by best friend Wednesday and a few other ladies, whom I've come to know through us all being worship leaders for dinner at Benihana. I walk into the restaurant and the hostess says I can look around for them. Turning the corner, I hear their laughter.

"What's up ladies?" I say laying my things down to give them a hug.

"You smell good girl, what is that?"

"Bubble Bistro of course. I mixed their body slushes, oil and body butter in the scents of pomegranate, black sugar and lick me. I keep telling y'all to stop sleeping on them. Their line of all-natural skin food is amazing."

"Well you sho smell good enough to lick," Wednesday laughs causing all of us to join in.

"Hey, I'm Yolanda, what can I get you to drink?"

"I'll have a strawberry Hennessey and water, please. Have y'all ordered appetizers?"

"Yes."

"Can I also get the beef gyoza dumplings?" I ask Yolanda.

"Sure thing. I'll put this in and be right back with your drinks."

"Okay Miss. Thang, what's going on with you and Pastor Gray?" Lailah asks.

"How did—" I cut my eye at Ari.

She sips her drink. "You know I got eyes everywhere and they told me how you showed up and shut the church down a few Sundays ago."

I shake my head. "I didn't expect to sing, I was only visiting because he invited me."

"Go on," they say.

I exhale. "We met on the plane to Jamaica, ate together a few times and now we're getting to know each other. We've been out a couple of times to see where things could potentially go. That's it."

"Dang, you move quick. Didn't his wife die like six months ago?" the new chick asks, and my eyebrows go up.

Chapter 14

"I'm sorry, what's your name again?" I question her.

"Genesis."

"Genesis, pretty name but his wife died over a year ago, but what does that have to do with me getting to know him?"

"I'm just saying. I wouldn't want my husband moving on so quick after I died."

"First, how would you know? And second, is he supposed to stop living too?" I quiz as Yolanda sits my drinks down.

"It's not about knowing, it's respect. You should be giving him space to grieve."

"Respect for who?" Ari asks. "His wife is gone, she ain't thinking about what her husband is doing and grief doesn't stop because you move on."

"Right," Wednesday adds. "Besides, him exploring a new relationship isn't disrespecting his marriage to the first wife. She died, not him and we don't know what the two of them talked about before. Not that you need permission Chance but do you sis and him when the time comes," she tips her glass to me.

"I'm not judging you," Genesis asserts, "I'm only stating my opinion. I just think it would be weird and uncomfortable to be in a person's house whose wife just died. Her clothes are probably still hanging in the closet and the house smells like her but do you."

"Yes, you're definitely judging," I tell her, "but it's cool and doesn't bother me, you're entitled to your opinion. However, I plan to do me and if God leads me to Mason, I'm not mad about it. You can be, but I won't."

"You didn't have to get smart," she huffs.

"Okay, you need to chill Genesis." Lailah voices. "We don't do all that here. We come together as adult sister friends who are capable of having conversations, stating our opinions and calling each other out on our mess, but it's the tone in your voice for me."

"I'm sorry," she states rolling her eyes. "I didn't realize y'all were easily offended."

"Okay you're pushing it," Wednesday exclaim. "I invited you because you're new to the scene of worship leaders but maybe we aren't the right fit for you."

"Oh, so now since I disagree with one thing, I don't fit this little Kumbaya group?" she laughs.

I take a sip of my drink. "You're missing the point of this little Kumbaya group, one you asked to be a part of. It's not about disagreeing because we don't always agree, it's your judgmental ass tone. Everybody at this table has opinions, however you don't know me to criticize my relationship."

"Well, we did see you baring it all, in your last relationship over the internet," she chuckles.

"And I was cute too, don't forget that but damn sis, you act like I screwed your man," I reply. "With all this animosity, is there something you need to get off your chest?"

"You really don't know who I am?" she asks with a stun expression.

"Should I?"

"I'm Jeff's wife," she matter-of-factly states.

The ladies all look at each other.

"Okay and that should mean what to me? Jeff is an ex and I've moved on. Whether Mason is my next is yet to be seen but even as a friend, he's everything Jeff wasn't."

"Then why won't you leave him alone?"

"Hold that thought," I reply when Yolanda sits our appetizers down and we place our dinner order. Wednesday says the grace for the table.

I pop a dumpling in my mouth. "You said what now?" I ask Genesis.

"I said for you to leave my husband alone."

"It's clear you have me confused with somebody else sweetie. Jeff can't even take my garbage out let alone be close enough for me to mess with."

"Then why are you texting him?"

"Can y'all explain things in simpler terms for her because it's obvious she doesn't understand my choice of language and I refuse to spend my night out talking about Jeff's rancid ass."

She pulls her phone and slides it over to me, showing screenshots of messages. "Isn't that your name?"

I use my napkin to turn the phone around then slide it back. "Girl I'm going to say this for the last time, I'm not fooling with, talking to or texting Jeff. He's a liar, manipulator and cheater whose number has been blocked in my phone since November. However, I find it ironic you were judging my relationship with Mason when you probably got the husband you currently have while he was with someone else."

"Who was alive," Wednesday adds.

She rolls her eyes and puffs her chest out. "Then why is your name and number in his phone."

"Lower your voice," Ari says.

"Did you dial the number?"

"What?" she gripes, irritated.

"Did you dial the number?" I repeat slowly. "See, I'm willing to bet that number is tied to the next victim of Jeff's even though it's my name. Yet, you didn't have the guts to dial it because you know it isn't me. The only reason you confronted me here, you're hoping I wouldn't drag you in public. I won't, not this time."

"And if this was the only reason you wanted to hang out with us, consider your future invitations rescinded. As a matter of fact," Ari says pulling out her phone, "let me go ahead and remove you from our group text."

"Yolanda," Lailah flags her down. "Cancel chick's order. Genesis, don't even worry about your drink and appetizer, I got it and you need to go."

"So, y'all are really taking up for her when she's cheating with my husband. What kind of women are you?"

I swallow my dumpling. "The kind that's trying to keep from whooping your ass in public. Look Genesis, I wouldn't touch Jeff if his blood could cure cancer. Whomever he's cheating with, it isn't me. However, karma always comes to collect and if he was cheating when he got with you, he's probably cheating on you. Maybe you should have started, you know like your name means, in the beginning getting to know Jeff and his antics. He may look like a gift, but he's really gutter trash. Now, grab your off-brand Birkin and gone because you're killing the vibe."

She snatches her phone and purse, stomping off.

"We didn't know," Wednesday assures.

"It's cool, but next time y'all want to invite someone to the group, don't." I tell them to laughter.

Getting home, I arm the alarm, grab a bottle of water from the refrigerator before taking a shower, turning on the bedside light and climbing into bed. A few minutes later, my phone vibrates with a Facetime call from Mason.

"Hey babe, did I catch you at a bad time?" he asks.

"No, I just got into bed. How are you?"

"I'm good. How was your night out with the ladies?"

"It was going great until I was confronted by Jeff's new wife, Genesis."

"Wait, come again."

"Apparently, she reached out to Wednesday saying she was new to the area and a worship leader, so they invited her to join us. I didn't know her, and Jeff has made her think him and I are fooling around."

"Are you?"

"I didn't hear you right. Repeat your question."

"I only asked for clarification purposes."

"You really think I'd go back to Jeff, the same man who used and dumped me and is currently married?"

"No, I'd hope not."

"Interesting. Goodnight Mason."

I release the call, putting the phone on do not disturb. Turning off the light, I play my worship playlist and slide under the covers.

"Lord, this is why I didn't want to try another relationship," I exhale. "Yet your will not mine."

Chapter 15

It's been a few days since I've talked to Mason, not for his lack of trying but I'm at a point where I'm no longer explaining myself to people who should know me. The three months I had to work on me gave me strength to confirm who I am and to be picky about who and what I deal with. Yes, I like Mason but not at the expense of losing me again.

I pull into my driveway after work and the grocery store, letting the garage down. Walking into the house, I drop my bags on the kitchen table and make a few trips to get the groceries. Kicking my shoes off, I wash my hands and begin to put everything away, except for what I'm cooking. Ribeye steak alfredo. I marinate my steak while I shower and change clothes.

Thirty minutes later, I put a pot of water on for the pasta and start to make my sauce when the doorbell rings.

"Ugh," I say turning the fire off under the sauce. Peeking out the window, I sigh when I see Mason on my doorstep.

"I apologize for showing up unannounced," he says as soon as I open the door.

"Mason, what can I do for you?" I ask after letting him inside.

"Chance, I'm sorry. I never should have questioned your relationship or lack thereof with Jeff. You told me things were over and instead I allowed jealousy to rear its head. I was having a bad night and I shouldn't have taken it out on you. I apologize if I hurt you."

"No, you shouldn't but you know Mason, I'm so sick of hearing folk apologize for things that could have been avoided. I'm tired of being treated like my freaking feelings don't matter and I will no longer explain myself to you or anybody else for however you feel about whatever. I thank you for the apology, but please go."

"Ch—"

"Please," I say opening the door.

He pauses in front of me kissing me on the cheek. I close the door, arm the alarm and go back to the kitchen to finish my dinner.

Two weeks later, I walk into Hyatt Regency. Wednesday convinced me to sing with her at a banquet for a local pastor and wife anniversary. When we're done, I grab my things and head out. I've had a long day and a headache which is getting worse. Walking towards the exit, I hear Mason call my name.

"Hey," he says giving me a hug. "You look great. Are you okay?"

"Hey, thanks and yes, I have a headache." I stumble a little and he catches me.

"Chance are you sure you're okay?"

"It's only a headache. I'm headed home to lay down."

"Will you allow me to drive you? I'd feel more comfortable making sure you get home instead of letting you drive like this. I can let Marcy drive my car once the banquet is over and I can take yours. Please let me do this for you."

"Okay," I reply sitting in a nearby chair.

"I'll be right back."

I have my eyes closed when he returns. "Let's get you home."

Mason pulls my car into the garage and lets it down. He nudges me.

"You're home."

I nod at him but don't move. He comes around opening the door.

"Babe, what's the code to the alarm?"

"0998," I mumble walking down the hall. I kick off my shoes and remove my dress and tights, sliding under the covers. I didn't even bother to turn on the light.

"Chance," I hear him say. "What do you need?"

"There's a pen in the refrigerator called emgality. It has to be left out for thirty minutes. If you can leave it on the nightstand, I'll inject it when I get up."

Sometime later, I hear Mason's voice, but I can't open my eyes.

"I'm going to give you your medicine."

I groan with tears sliding from my eyes.

"One, two, three," he says.

When I open my eyes, there's something over them. I move it and realize it's a towel. Staring at the ceiling, it registers that I'm at home. I look over and it's still dark out. Sitting up, I groan and throw the cover back to go to the restroom. Finished and after cleaning my face, I wrap my robe around me and open the door.

Walking into the kitchen, the time on the stove is 3:57 AM.

I grab a bottle of water from the refrigerator, open and put it to my mouth.

"Hey, are you feeling better?"

"Aw," I scream dropping the bottle. "Oh my God Mason, you scared me."

He rushes to get it before a lot of the water spills. "I'm sorry, I was trying not to. I thought it would be better to say something than to touch you."

"Lord," I take a few deep breaths. "I was not expecting you to be here."

"There was no way I could leave you like that. You were in so much pain. Do you get headaches like that often?"

"I used too, but I hadn't had one like this in a long time. It didn't feel as bad until after I sung. You gave me the shot?" I ask when I see the paper in the garbage.

"Yes, you were in no shape to give it to yourself."

I smile. "Thank you. I don't remember much after getting home so I appreciate you for being here. I hope I didn't mess up your night."

"You didn't. In fact, you saved me from another banquet of roast beef, mashed potatoes, green beans and sweet tea." We say the menu together before laughing.

"Seriously," he says, "are you feeling better?"

"Yes, I am and I'm very appreciative to you for taking care of me. I don't know how I would have made it home without you."

"Anything for you."

"It's still early and I would fix breakfast, as a way of showing my gratitude, but I'm going to lay down for a few more hours to ensure this headache is gone."

"It's fine, I told Marcy to pick me up after her 9 AM class, but if you're not comfortable with me being here, I'll get an Uber."

"I'm not uncomfortable around you Mason," I assure him. "However, I'm not your problem."

"You're nobody's problem Chance and I know this isn't the time but I'm sorry for the way I acted towards you." He walks closer to me. "These last few weeks without speaking and seeing you have been hard, and I can't go on like this. Then seeing you in pain last night, Chance, please forgive me. Let me be here to take care of you so that you never have to worry about getting home or having your medicine when you're sick. Forgive me so I can show you what a real man looks, feels, loves and taste like. Forgive me so I can make you the wife and mother you're destined to be. Chance, will you give me another chance with your heart?"

"I'm sorry Mason but I can't."

Chapter 16

He sighs, turning to walk off.

"You didn't allow me to finish," I say. "I can't rush into this. I like you and it was hard to hear you question my feelings for Jeff. I felt like I was back in Jamaica with my family being judged about the choices I make." I put my hand up to stop him from walking any closer. "No, wait. You're saying and doing all the right things, you're here when I need you and that makes my heart leap. However, my heart has leapt before and it ended in the wrong hands. I can't make that mistake again."

"Can we start over?"

"I'm 40 years old and sick of starting over, let's just start getting it right. Mason, I'm not perfect in life or relationships, but I know what I don't want and that's to be hurt again. If you're having any doubts about trusting me, then don't. I'd rather be alone than to keep going through this."

"I hear you and again, I apologize for making you feel untrustworthy and trusting of me with your heart. I will be honest and tell you that I'm not perfect and I may mess up, yet I'll never intentionally break your heart if you allow me access to it. Chance, I'm not Jeff or the many others before him."

"Hold up, don't make me sound like a thot," I smile.

"Wrong choice of words," he laughs. "What I meant is, don't miss out on love because you've judged it by the failed attempts of the assholes before me. Baby, my name is Mason Jeremiah Gray and I'm willing to love you until my dying day. Will I mess up? Yes, but I pray not too many times. Will I break a promise? Probably, but I pray not too many times. Will I love you beyond the hurt and brokenness of yesterday? Yes, for as long as you allow me too."

I exhale. "This seems to real to be true."

"God is too yet you trust Him, don't you?"

"Yeah, but you aren't God."

"I'm made in His image though," he smirks. "That should give me some credit."

I laugh and shake my head. "I can't with you."

"Will you give us another chance?"

I pause before answering. "Yes Mason. I'll give us another chance."

He rushes over to me, grabbing my face and pulling me in for a passionate kiss. "Okay, I'm going to let you go back to your bedroom before we commit a sin. Cause child the spirit is willing, but my flesh is getting weak."

I walk away.

"Mason, thank you for taking care of me."

"You're welcome. Oh, your friend Wednesday called last night. I hope you don't mind that I answered but she was calling and texting by the time I got your purse out the car and I didn't want her to worry."

"It's cool. I'll call her in a little while."

I go into my bedroom and close the door. Kneeling beside the bed, I bow my head to pray.

"Okay God, if Mason is who you have for me, thank you because you are showing out for your girl. Seriously, guide me so that I don't make another mistake with my flesh. Hide my heart within you that He'll have to get your permission to enter it. Father, it's only been a few months and although I know you can work quick, don't let me move outside of your will. I like Mason and I know it'll be easy to love him, but only with your permission. Don't let me move by only the desires of flesh because I've done that too many times and messed up. This time, your will God and not mine. And God, thank you for sparing my life on last night and for him being here when I needed it. Amen."

A few hours later Mason taps on the door. I'm already up showered and dressed and sitting in the chair in front of my bedroom window.

"Hey, I hope I'm not disturbing you."

"No, come in. I'm listening to this song Wednesday sent me."

"Marcy is here to pick me up and she wanted to know if you'll join us for dinner tonight."

"Sure, I'd like that."

"I'll pick you up about 6:30."

"Sounds great."

I lay my notebook and phone down, getting up to walk him to the door. He kisses me on the lips.

"I'll see you later."

"Hey," Mason says when I open the door. "You look beautiful as always."

"Thank you and so do you."

I lock up before walking to the passenger side of his truck. He holds the door while I get in.

"Good evening Ms. Chance," Marcy says from the back seat.

"Hey Marcy and please call me Chance."

"Are you ladies ready for dinner?" Mason asks when he gets in.

"Yes, and I hope you're taking us somewhere nice," Marcy states.

"As a matter of fact, I thought we could do dinner at Como Steakhouse. It's about a 45-minute drive, but worth it. Is that okay with you both?"

"As long as I can control the music," I tell him.

"Marcy?" Mason looks in the rearview mirror.

"I'm cool with that and I have my headphones in case y'all play old people music."

"Oh no she didn't," I say laughing while pulling out my phone and playing California Love by Tupac.

"Aw, girl what you know bout Pac," Mason exclaims.

By the time we arrive at the steak house we've had a DJ party on wheels.

"Okay," Marcy says shaking her head, "you did good and please share that playlist with me."

"Oh, it wasn't too old for you?" I laugh, handing her my phone as we're walking in.

After dinner, Mason walks me to the door. Marcy is asleep in the back seat.

"Thank you for another amazing dinner."

He kisses me on the cheek. "The next time, it's just you and me."

"Deal. Goodnight Mason."

"Sweet dreams Chance."

I go inside the house, praying tonight doesn't end like it did after our night in Jamaica. I arm the alarm and float to my bedroom. Falling back on the bed, my phone vibrates. Scared to look, I lift it over my face to see a text from Wednesday.

My Girl Wednesday: How was the date (with the eyes emoji).

"Thank God," I exclaim sitting up to reply.

Me: It was amazing. Sis, is it too early to fall in love?

She calls. I answer and put it on speaker. She doesn't even say hello.

"Girl, where in the Bible does it say there's a time limit to fall in love? Cause I'm flipping through the good book ret now and I don't see it."

I laugh.

"Seriously Chance, you're forty years old and have been through your fair share of messed up relationships. I don't blame you for not wanting to waste any more time when there's a fine, God fearing, fine, black man who knows what he wants and that's you. Did I mention he's fine?"

"Uh yeah, a few times."

"Okay good, didn't want you to miss that."

"I don't want to mess this up though. I really like him and his daughter Wednesday. I mean, it's not every day a girl, who's the dad's new girlfriend after losing her mom, can get along with a teenager. Did I include the fact her mom has only been gone a year? What if I can't be what they need?"

"What if you can? You're allowing fear to talk you out of your blessing. Stop it. That man has been telling you for months you're his wife and unlike stinky Jeff, he has God's ear. I'm pretty sure he wouldn't be this confident if you being his wife wasn't part of God's plan for his life."

"I hear you."

"Psalm thirty-seven and twenty-three, *"the Lord directs the steps of the Godly. He delights in every detail of their lives."* Chance, since you returned from Jamaica you've been rebuilding your relationship and trust in God, right?"

"Yeah."

“Then trust Him sis. I love you.”

“I love you too.”

“Now tell me about the date,” she says.

Chapter 17

June

Over the last two months, Mason and I date as we get to know each other, and it feels like I've known him for years. I thank God every day for answering my prayers because I had closed my heart to love, but God didn't. I've also had the opportunity to build a relationship with Marcy.

Although Mason and I haven't had an official conversation, we are exclusive and I'm falling deeper in love with him daily. Things have been going so well that sometimes I find my mind wandering, thinking this is too good to be true but then David's word in Psalm forty reminds me of God's power.

David says in verses one through five, *"I waited patiently for the LORD to help me, and he turned to me and heard my cry. He lifted me out of the pit of despair, out of the mud and the mire. He set my feet on solid ground and steadied me as I walked along. He has given me a new song to sing, a hymn of praise to our God. Many will see what he has done and be amazed. They will put their trust in the LORD. Oh, the joys of those who trust the LORD, who have no confidence in the proud or in those who worship idols. O LORD my God, you have performed many wonders for us. Your plans for us are too numerous to list. You have no equal. If I tried to recite all your wonderful deeds, I would never come to the end of them."*

"Ma'am are you looking for someone?" a young man asks pulling me from my thoughts.

"No, I'm waiting. He should be here any moment."

I'm standing in the foyer of Hope Christian Center waiting on Mason to walk in. He has to preach tonight and asked me to sing a solo. When the door opens, I turn to see Genesis. She looks me up and down and I smile knowing I'm rocking the black pencil skirt that touches right below my knees, a deep blue belted blazer and black pumps.

"Just speak sis and keep it moving."

She chuckles before walking around the corner.

"Babe, my apology for keeping you waiting," Mason rushes in.

"No problem, you okay?"

"Yeah, my computer was acting crazy, so I had to ensure it was good before I left the house."

"I told you to replace that thing."

"I know," he takes my hand as we walk to the Pastor's office. "After tonight, it'll be the first thing I do in the morning."

Turning the corner, we pass Jeff and Genesis who seem to be in the middle of a heated discussion.

"Pastor Gray," Pastor Dillard says when we get to the door. "Son, it's good to see you again."

"You too, sir. Allow me to introduce you to my Chance."

I hear Jeff suck in air behind me.

"I finally get to meet this songbird and soon to be bride of my dearest son in the ministry. He talks about you a lot."

"I've heard," I smile looking at Mason. "Pastor Dillard, it's nice to finally meet you too."

Genesis clears her throat.

"Reverend and Mrs. Walker," he says to Jeff, "how are you two this evening?"

"We're fine sir."

"Babe, I'm going to go out and get a seat." I say to Mason.

"No need," Pastor Dillard says. "I have a seat for you. Now, let us have a word of prayer before we go out."

We all grab hands.

"God, we thank you for another chance to gather in your holy temple. We ask that you release the Holy Spirit to fall so that men and women may be saved, chains destroyed, and deliverance released. Use your servant leader Mason to break unto us the bread of life and Chance as she ministers through song. Give them power to profess your glory as you see fit. Bless this house and ministry with all we stand in need of. Let tonight be whatever you'll have it to be. This we pray, amen."

I face Mason. "Do what God has anointed you to do," he tells me.

"You do the same boo."

He kisses me on the lips before we all walk into the sanctuary.

I stop by the musician to let him know what I'd be singing and when it's my turn, my stomach is a ball of nerves. No matter how many times I do this, I never fail to be nervous. I look over at Mason who smiles.

I take a deep breath as the choir stands and the music begins.

"I've got so much to thank God for. So many wonderful blessings and so many open doors. A brand-new mercy along with each new day that's why I praise you and for this I give You praise. For waking me up this morning. For starting me on my way. For letting me see the sunshine of a brand-new day. For grace and mercy to give to me today. For this I give you praise."

By the time I'm done, the choir is in full worship. Getting to my seat, they start back up and Mason passes me the microphone.

"You're Jehovah Jireh. You've been my provider. So many times, you met my need, so many times you rescued me. For the blessings you give to me each day, that's why I praise you." I belt before speaking in tongue. "Thank you, Jesus. Is there anyone else in the house tonight thankful to God for the mountains He's brought us over? Anybody else grateful for the many things God blocked? Anybody else got a praise for the doors God shut and the ones He's opened. Yeah Lord,

I give you praise. You're Jehovah Jireh. You've been my provider. So many times, you met my need, so many times you rescued me. For the blessings you give to me each day, that's why I praise you."

I push the microphone back to Mason.

"Oh, come on somebody and tell the Lord thank you," Mason bellows in the microphone. "When you can worship God on a Thursday night because you're in your right mind, somebody ought to have a praise. When you can lift up your hands all by yourself, that should be enough to tell God thank you. Can we praise God tonight, church?"

A few more minutes later, the congregation has settled enough for Mason to take his text and me to step out to the bathroom. Coming out, Jeff is standing there.

"You're getting married?" he questions.

"Um, hi, hello. Whether I am or not is none of your concern."

"I only asked."

I move pass him.

"You sounded great tonight. Glad to see you moved passed everything that happened and started singing again. For now," he adds.

"What is that supposed to mean?"

"Come on Chance. You don't think Pastor Gray," he mockingly says, "is going to allow you to keep singing like that."

I chuckle. "Allow me? Naw dude, allow me to explain something to you, reverend," I return the ridicule. "My boo isn't threatened by my gift, my strength or my glory because he's a real man. See, we don't compete. Instead we've linked our faith to contribute to God's kingdom as one. You'd never know anything about that because you're a simple, selfish, shameful, short nature Negro who wants the glory. With you, there's no room for anybody else. I only pray

you get the healing you need before you break your new wife's heart and spirit."

Turning to walk away, Genesis is standing there.

"Good luck sweetie," I tell her, "and I hope you don't allow him to muzzle you."

Chapter 18

After church Mason and I stop to get dinner at Applebee's.

"When I went out to the bathroom after singing, I saw Jeff," I tell Mason as we're enjoying boneless buffalo wings. "He had the nerve to compliment my singing then says, enjoy it for now."

"What does that mean?" he asks concerned.

I lay my fork down. "He said it wouldn't be long before you stopped me from singing. No, I'm sorry as that wasn't his choice of words. He said you wouldn't allow me."

"That dude doesn't know me. Babe, I'd never stop you from using that big, bold gift you have. Tonight, you caused worship to happen and there's no way I'll stand in the way of that. Neither is it my place to allow you to do anything. You're a grown, anointed, smart, soulful, sexy, chocolate woman who I happen to love."

"You love me?" I blush.

"Girl, I've loved you from the moment you jumped into my arms on that boat. I'm simply waiting in expectation of you loving me back."

"I do love you Mason and I apologize for taking this long to tell you. If I can be truthful. I think I loved you from that moment too. You took the time to take me away from the drama of my family and celebrate my birthday after knowing me for 24 hours. Even after listening to all my mess."

"No," he says grabbing my hand and motioning for me to join him on his side of the booth. "Don't you dare apologize for taking the time you needed. I know you love me, and I knew it was a matter of time for your mouth to catch up to your heart."

"I don't want to mess this up. I've never felt like this before."

"Then don't. Let us walk this thang together, each day being for one another what God has ordained. We may make mistakes but as long as we're willing, we'll make it."

I grab his face and kiss him.

"Now, how long do I have to wait to propose?" he inquires.

I look at him.

"I'm serious Chance. I've been granted an opportunity to find love twice in my lifetime and I'm not passing it up. You will be my wife, sooner than later. Although I won't rush you, could you make it quick?"

"I'm ready when you are," I admit.

"Girl, don't play with me because I'll book a red eye to Vegas and we'll be married by morning."

I laugh. "Maybe not Vegas, but I'm for real."

"Let me get the check?" he says.

"Babe, there's nothing we can do tonight. Besides, I want my tacos."

He looks at me and smiles. "Fine. Get your stinking tacos."

I kiss him again.

An hour later, we're walking to our cars.

"Mason, you don't think this is crazy, do you? It's been seven months."

"Chance, if you're not ready I'm willing to wait for you. However, no I don't think it's crazy. A woman who is seven months pregnant can deliver a baby, although premature it has the potential to survive with the right medical help and prayers. In seven months, I can have a house built from the ground up and seven biblically is perfection and completeness. Again, I'm not trying to convince you because I get that you're scared. When you're ready, my faux proposal stands."

He opens my car door, kisses me on the lips and waits until I get in.

"Call me when you get home."

"Yes sir."

Getting home, I don't get no further than the living room before I burst into tears. I slide down on my knees.

"God, please move me out of the way before I sabotage who and what you have for me. God, I know I've messed up in the past by moving too fast. I gave my heart to those whose hearts I didn't even have, but don't allow me to miss my husband because of me. I've been praying for love and I can't miss it because of my mistakes. I've been yearning for love, don't let flesh talk me out of it. Father, I believe but help my unbelief. Then forgive me for continually asking for a sign when it's been in front of me this entire time. If you allow me to wake up in the morning, I vow to not take another minute for granted."

Two days later, ringing of my doorbell wakes me. I look at the clock and groan because it's rare I sleep in on Saturday. I get up, pull my robe on and shuffle down the hall.

"Who is it?" I ask.

"It's your dad."

I roll my eyes. Unarming the alarm, I open the door.

"Dad, what are you doing here?"

"Button, can we talk?"

"Sure."

I let him in and tell him to give me a few to change clothes. Thirty minutes later, I join him in the living room.

"Can we talk in the kitchen because I need coffee?"

He nods. Sitting at the island, he watches me as I grab two cups from the cabinet. "You still take yours black?"

"Yes."

"What's up dad?" I question once I'm standing across from him after making our coffees and handing him his cup.

"I'm sorry for showing up at your house unannounced but I miss you. I know it doesn't mean much, at this moment and before you kick me out, I wanted you to know I've left your mom."

"I hope you don't expect me to jump into your arms with joy. You all condoned her hatred of me for my entire life and a divorce now means absolutely nothing to me."

"I know it's a small drop in the bucket compared to what you've gone through, but after Jamaica I realized the fool I've been for the majority of your life. I knew Camilla didn't like my mom and vice versa and I should have taken you and left the moment she mentioned putting you up for adoption. However, I thought it was a phase because she's your mother. Then as time went on, I kept making excuses saying she'll love you when you call her mommy, when you wrapped your arms around her—"

"Yet, year after year none of those things worked and as my father you allowed her to mistreat me. Sorry doesn't make that go away. No matter how many I love you text you send or the number of times you call me button, the fact still remains you didn't protect me. I'm your oldest daughter."

"I know," he sighs.

"You know," I scream. "Well, your knowing didn't soothe the many years of feeling abandoned nor the countless nights, I had to spend alone while y'all had family time, I wasn't invited too. Do you know how many messed up relationships I've allowed myself to be mistreated in because I was looking for the affection my dad took back? Don't get me wrong, I have a lot of blame for that too, but you're supposed to show me how a man is supposed to love a woman. When God trusted you with me, He designed it for you to teach me what to expect from a man. You're supposed to be the first living man I trust in and you let me down."

"Button—"

"Stop calling me that," I angrily tell him. "You gave me that name when I was three because you said you and I were as tight and secure as the buttons on a shirt. It may have worked then but it's always been a lie. When I needed you to fasten the holes in my heart, caused by your wife, you didn't," I scream.

"It wasn't a lie," he cries, "but I failed you. I put the heart of my wife before you. I'm sorry for allowing you to be cast away and not protecting you. God knows I should have said and done something before now. Please forgive me Chance. I miss you," he sobs. "I miss your early morning phone calls and your texts throughout the day. I miss the lunches we shared on Sundays and your hugs. I'll do whatever it takes to fix our relationship. Is there anywhere in your heart to give your old man another chance because I don't think I can go on if you don't?"

"No, you don't get to put that guilt on me. God," I yell. "I'm not the reason we're in the shape we are. You were the adult, not me. You were the one who should have—you know what, I'm not going to continue to do this. I did all those things with you because I love you and I thought you loved me too.”

“I didn’t mean it that way and I do love you. I just need my button back. Please Chance,” he pleads. “Please forgive me.”

I stand there stoic until I hear, “forgive him,” so loud in my ears that I drop the cup.

“Chance.”

I rush into my bedroom, closing the door while shaking my head no. “After everything, you want me to forgive that easily? They hurt me,” I yell. “God, he hurt me.”

“You’ve hurt me and yet I forgive you,” I hear clearly.

I stop in my tracks.

I shake my head no again. “No, no. He’s my dad. He should have protected me.” I go into the bathroom, turning around in circles. “God,” I scream. “You can’t expect me to do this after everything that’s been done to me. You know how they treated me, and he allowed it. He allowed it," I scream again.

I freeze when writing appears on the mirror.

Isaiah 43:18-19

I rush to get my Bible from the nightstand. Flipping the pages, I begin to read out loud.

"But forget all that— it is nothing compared to what I am going to do. For I am about to do something new. See, I have already begun! Do you not see it? I will make a pathway through the wilderness. I will create rivers in the dry wasteland."

"How am I supposed to forget it, just as quickly as I take a breath?" I ask God pressing the Bible against my chest. "How?"

"By giving grace."

I slump on the bed as tears pour from my eyes. Closing them, God allows me to taste my words from last night.

If you allow me to wake up in the morning, I vow to not take another minute for granted.

Chapter 19

It takes another fifteen minutes of me bantering with God before I lose and have to get myself together. I walk into the kitchen and dad stands.

"You okay?"

"Yeah," I somberly answer. "I hope my screaming didn't scare you."

He looks at me confusedly. "I didn't hear you scream. Did something happen?"

"You—I—never mind," I shake my head.

"I cleaned up the coffee, but I didn't know how to work that fancy machine to make you another cup."

"It's okay," I tell him. "Have a seat."

I sit next to him.

"The flesh of me doesn't want to forgive you dad. Truth is, I want you to hurt and miss me like I've hurt and missed you all these years even though you were right here. Those lunches and phone calls felt like you and I were close but as soon as they were over, you were gone," I exhale. "I want you to feel pain as I have knowing I've had to pay for the sins of my mother. Hearing the things mom said cut parts of me I didn't even realized words could reach. For your own mother to hate you, it's something that never sits right, and I tried to make it make sense then I stopped. It took some time, after coming home from Jamaica and crying for weeks straight, but I put you all out of my head and moved on. To me, y'all don't deserve me. But I have to forgive all of you because God has so graciously forgiven me, especially when I didn't deserve it."

"Thank you," he replies wiping his face. "Thank you." He gets up and wraps his arms around me. I hesitate then I hug him back.

"Things can't go back to the way they were, but I'm willing to see where they go from here. With you," I clarify.

He nods, pulling me into him again.

"I have a lot to make up for," he tells me.

"No, you can't, and I don't expect you too. Start from right now being a better dad because no matter how old I am, I still need and love you. If I didn't, I would have slammed the door in your face."

"I'm right here."

He hugs me one last time and I get up to make fresh coffee.

"Did you really leave mom?"

"As fast as the repo man leaves after snatching your car."

"Wait, what?" I laugh.

"It was long overdue."

"That I agree with," I add.

"I know it isn't Sunday, but can we start with lunch?" he asks.

"Yes, I'd like that."

Sunday Morning

I walk into Harvest Tabernacle and after being greeted, hugged and given peppermints, I tap on Mason's door that's ajar.

"Come in," he says. "Good morning."

"Hey, just letting you know I was here. Do you need anything before I go into the sanctuary?"

"Only a hug."

"That I can do."

"Hmm, you smell good. That Bubble Bistro is going to get me in trouble."

"Let me go," I chuckle. "Preach well this morning Pastor Gray and," I say stop at the door. "I'm ready to be your wife."

"Hold up," he rushes over, pulling me back inside. "Repeat yourself woman."

"Thank you for being willing to wait. Thank you for being willing to love me through my insecurities about relationships. Thank you for being you, but I'm ready now. Mason, I'm ready to be your wife."

"Are you sure?"

"If I could show you the intricate details of my heart then you'd know I am. I love you."

He looks at me without saying anything.

"Are you going to say something?"

"Hush woman, I'm trying to calculate how many days it'll take to get our marriage license."

"Man, goodbye. I'll see you after service."

After devotion, I join the choir to lead Oh How Precious. Getting ready to walk back to my seat, Mason grabs my hand.

"Good morning HTP. God is a mighty good Father, isn't He? Whenever you need Him, He's there. Whenever you try Him, He'll come through. Whenever you test Him, He'll past it every time. When Mallory was diagnosed with cancer, I trusted God. When the chemotherapy and drugs no longer worked, I trusted

God. When she became too sick to whisper my name, I trusted God. When she passed away, I trusted God. See, here's what I've come to understand. Through all of that, God hadn't let me down. Even the many nights I'd stand outside the room she was no longer in, I trusted Him with all of me because I knew He'd never let me down. A few nights before I left for Jamaica, God woke me up with the word chance. He told me there'd be another chance for me to love. Days later, I met this woman, named Chance, on the plane and this morning, she accepted becoming my wife."

The congregation cheers and I wipe the tears that were already falling.

He holds his hand up to quiet them. "I know somebody maybe saying it's too soon, well ma'am or sir, take it up with God because He's the controller of this heart. I pray you all will continue to treat Chance with respect, accepting her as the new Lady of HTP and as my wife. I pray you all will love on her as she becomes a bigger part of this family. Oh, just so you know there will not be a long courtship. I'm too old to be somebody's boyfriend, God made me husband material. Is that okay with you Ms. Chance?"

"It absolutely is."

He kisses me on the lips and I take my seat. My phone vibrates with a message from Marcy.

Marcy: I'm so happy for you and dad and I love you Chance.

Me: I love you too.

My Girl Wednesday: Bout freaking time!!!!!!!

Me: How do you even know?

My Girl Wednesday: The live stream, duh! Congrats boo.

Me: Thanks chick.

A little later, I walk down to the altar for prayer. I feel someone grab my hand and I look to my left to see my dad. I smile, gripping his hand.

“Congratulations Button.”

“Thank you, daddy.”

Chapter 20

September 20, 2020

I'm standing in the office, that will be mine, at the church fidgeting with my dress. Today is my wedding day and although it's my first wedding, I didn't want a traditional wedding gown. Instead I opted for a burgundy, floor length dress and of course the bottom is sequin and so are the cuff of the sleeves. Mason and I went through six weeks of premarital counseling with Pastor Dillard and his wife before settling on this date. We also both had physicals done and handled all of our financial business.

We decided to sell both of our houses. Mason's was put on the market first and yesterday, he accepted an offer. After the wedding, he's going to move into my house until we can find and close on our new home. As for now, it's time for me to become Mrs. Chance Gray.

I go over to the desk to find some paper to spit this peppermint in.

Opening the middle drawer, there's an envelope with "New First Lady," written on it. I open it to see a flash drive.

"Babe," I hear Mason say, "can you come to the door please?"

I lay the envelope on the desk and walk over, taking his hand that's extended through it.

"Dear God, thank you. Your word says a man who finds a wife finds a good thing and obtains favor from the Lord. Well Father, you've allowed me to find favor a second time and for that I'm extremely grateful. Now, I ask you to bless our union of becoming one. Give us strength to overcome what tries to stumble us, approach for what tries to attack us, provisions for what you're sending us to birth and a satisfying appetite for each other that never dwindles. Father, this is by your might and we can't do this alone. Sustain us. This we pray, amen."

I pull him towards me until his face is inside the door. "Boy, I'm getting you pregnant tonight."

"I can't wait," he says kissing me.

"That's what I'm talking bout," Wednesday says when I close the door.

"Girl, I didn't even hear you come in."

"That's because you were too busy talking nasty to the pastor."

I laugh.

"And was. Now, come on so I can hurry up and get home," I tell her licking my tongue out.

Standing at the entrance of the sanctuary, I grab my dad's arm as the song, Forever by Jason Nelson begins to play. Making it to the end of the aisle, I look at my dad who has tears streaming.

Pastor Dillard speaks, "Friends and family, we come together today in this sacred and holy place, to

witness the blending together of two flesh as they vow to one another a promise for the present as husband and wife. Who gives this woman to be married to this man?"

"I do," dad says kissing me on the cheek.

"Dearly beloved, we gather today under the hand of God, in His sight and in the presence of those invited to witness the uniting of Mason and Chance in holy matrimony. Recognizing the promise, you both make today is more than a legal contract. A marriage is a covenant agreement between man and woman who have intentionally vowed to be one with and for each other until death you two shall part. Is that your vow?"

"It is," Mason and I say.

"God's word gives us a commandment and I shall make it known to each of you today. Love one another. Despite what the flesh will make you believe, love can conquer all. When you're upset, remember you love each other. When things don't go your way, remember to love one another. When the enemy attacks and he will, remember to let love be your strength to overcome. When the naysayers talk, remember you love each other, and you've been given another chance. Bible says in First Corinthians thirteen, *"Love is patient and kind. Love is not jealous or boastful or proud or rude. It does not demand its own way. It is not irritable, and it keeps no record of being wronged. It does not rejoice about injustice but rejoices whenever the truth wins out. Love never gives up, never loses faith, is always hopeful, and endures through every circumstance."* Please join your right hands."

I've already started to cry. Pastor Dillard hands me the microphone and Mason looks shocked.

"Mason, I know we didn't decide to write our own vows, but I couldn't let this moment pass without saying this in front of our family and friends. Thank you for giving me another chance at love. Thank you for not staying away even when I pushed you. Thank you for showing me that love doesn't have a set amount of time. Thank you for seeing me. Thank you for giving me time and more importantly, thank you for giving me the chance to tell everybody that you're mine. At forty years old, I was willing to let go of love because I didn't think it was for me, you changed that. I'd closed my heart to love, but God didn't. You and Marcy accepted me and told me to be authentically me and I'm grateful. Harvest Tabernacle accepted me and I'm thankful. Love left me wounded and yet you came in with a first aid kit willing to stitch me up and now, I'm willing to love you for the rest of my life."

"That's how you get yo man sis," Wednesday whispers wiping my face.

Mason takes the microphone, "Chance baby, in taking your hand I am yours in body, spirit, deed and love. I make a vow before everybody that you are my good thing, my lawful, wedded wife and for you I will forsake all others. I promise to love, cherish, honor and endure you in sickness and in health and prosperity. I promise to be your rock to lean on in the good and especially when bad may darken your days. You are my second chance and I will love you for the rest of my life."

"Nothing more needs to be said," Pastor Dillard says. "May I have the rings? These rings symbolize the vow each of you have made. They are formed in a circle, sized to fit each of your finger as a symbolic reminder that love, although has a beginning, it should have no end. Repeat after me together. I give and take this ring as a token and pledge of my constant faith and abiding love from this day forward. This ring is the outward sign of the love my heart sings and it is therefore a bond uniting our hearts in love that has no end."

We go over and instead of lighting a unity candle, we fill a flask with two different color sand. The mixing together is our way of symbolizing the merging of our faith.

"Let us pray."

Mason and I kneel.

"God, we yet again thank you for what you've allowed to transpire in the lives of Mason and Chance. God, this union has been ordained by you, now God sanction it to be everlasting until you say well done. Cover and protect them from the work of evil that may already be spoken. Guide them so they never steer away from you. Connect them through faith, love, obedience and strength that they'll continually walk according to your ways for them. Bless this union, allow them to birth what you give permission too and let them speak and sing what the Holy Spirit gives utterance. We cover them in your grace and protection. Bind the hands of evilness so that it does not prosper. Father, we commit them to you and let no man pull asunder what you've connected. This we pray, amen."

He waits until we stand.

"Having pledged your faith and love for each other and sealing your vows by the exchanging of rings, I now by the power of a just and faithful God pronounce you husband and wife. What God has joined together, let not man or woman, evil, witch, warlock or worker of iniquity tear apart. You may kiss your good thang."

After the reception, Mason and I change clothes for our honeymoon. We're only taking a few days in the smoky mountains of Sevierville, TN because we're going back to Jamaica in November, a year to the date of when we met.

Getting into his truck, he leans over and kisses me.

"I love you Mrs. Gray."

"I love you too, Mr. Gray."

"Now, that thing you said about getting me pregnant," he smirks.

"Oh, I definitely meant that. Drive."

Chapter 21

Once Mason is asleep, I pull the envelope that I found at the church from my bag. Grabbing my laptop and Air Pods, I move to the living room. Plugging in the USB, the file explorer opens with a video. Clicking on it, it's Mallory.

"If you're watching this, it means Mason has asked you to become his wife and new Lady of Harvest Tabernacle. I hid this in the drawer during my last visit at the church. He doesn't know about it and you can choose to tell him, if you like. I only wanted to tell you to take care of him. He's a great man and he loves hard. I know it's rare, especially with him being in the ministry, but he's faithful," she chuckles before coughing. "Seriously, he is a great man, father and pastor. He's an even greater lover. Phew," she waves herself. "You'll see or maybe you have. Mason would turn red if he knew I told you that, but it's true."

She pauses before continuing. "We've been through a lot and watching me die is one of the hardest things. I can see it in his eyes although he tries to be strong. While I don't know how long it's been since I've been gone, and he's moved on, I pray it wasn't long. A man like Mason deserves to be loved. Will you give it to him? Will you love him, past me? Will you love him out of his grief?" She exhales. "I'm not going to cry. I only pray you'll get to experience more years with that man than me. Lastly, take care of my Marcy. I didn't tell her father, but she and I had this talk and I asked her to respect who her dad chooses. I know he'll make the right decision with you because he always goes with God and his heart. Oh, don't try to follow in my footsteps. Girl, I'm gone and you're the newest Mrs. Gray. Walk the way God leads. Last thing, for real, watch out for messy Henrietta and Elnora at the

church, they'll spread your business and don't let them guilt you into being on every board and program either. Just because you're first lady doesn't mean you have to be chained to that church every minute. Find a balance and enjoy it."

"Babe, what are you doing?" I hear Mason's voice in the video.

"Gotta go," she whispers. "And congratulations. You're going to be a great wife because Mason chose you."

"Babe, what are you doing?" I jump when I hear Mason's voice behind me. I quickly wipe the tears showing him the laptop.

"Wow," he says when it finishes. "I had no idea she made this, although I'm not surprised. Was she right?"

"About what?"

"Me being a great lover?"

"Really dude? Is that all you got from that?"

"Well, this was a video for you," he smirks.

I shake my head. "In order to effectively answer your question, I'll need more to gauge the results on." I get up and drop my robe.

Chapter 22

November

Mason and I finally moved into our new house two weeks ago. It was one we found that had everything we were looking for and the closing process was simple and easy. Today, I'm at my old house waiting on the painters as we prepare it to go on the market. I'm doing a final walk through when the doorbell rings.

"Come in," I say coming down the hall. "Jeff? What are you doing here?"

"Hey Chance."

"Hi, what's up?"

"I didn't realize you were moving? I've been out of town for a few months because I was hired as pastor of a church in Birmingham. It's smaller than what I wanted, but it'll do for now."

"You still haven't changed," I shake my head.

"Anyway, I heard you got married." He says ignoring my statement.

"I did."

"Look, I'm sorry for the way I handled things with us. I know it's a little too late, but I thought it was only right I made amends with you."

"Is this part of a twelve-step program? If so, it isn't working."

"See, why can't you just listen and let me say this," he belts.

"Hold on dude, take it down a notch. This whole amends thing is a little too late, it's been almost a year. So, what do you really want because there's always a hidden agenda with you?"

"Why can't you believe I've changed?"

"Whether you have or not, it's not my concern. I can only pray that said change benefits your new wife and church family. Now, if you'll excuse me."

"I only came for closure," he announces. "My marriage to Genesis has been pure hell and I probably deserve it for how I treated you. I threw everything we had out the window after three years because of my ego. I'm sorry Chance."

"Great, consider this book closed."

"Can we be friends?" he asks.

"Friends," I laugh really loud, "are you serious? No Jeff, we can't be friends, but I appreciate you wanting to apologize in person. As for you deserving what you're getting, you're right. You deserve all God is giving you for the despicable things you did to me. Nonetheless, I'm over it and you should be too. I have never wished any ill will towards you neither am I pining over what went wrong in our relationship. If I can be honest, I should thank you."

"Thank me?"

"Yes, thank you. It was your dumping that allowed me to see what I didn't want in a man and what we had wasn't real love. See, you dumping me when you did, led me to Jamaica alone. Being there I was finally able to get closure on why my family treated me like they did. Those pictures that were leaked, they taught me to love me, flaws and all. However, the best part, I was able to find my voice again and a man who loves me unconditionally. My husband was sitting one seat away from me on the plane and had you been there, I never would have seen him, so thank you. Thank you for not being able to see the woman I am and for moving out the way for the man I married who loves me deeply and makes great love to my mind, body and soul. Child, I get happy just thinking about his fine self."

"And baby you make me just as happy."

Jeff turns to the sound of Mason's voice who is standing in the door.

Mason extends his hand to Jeff. "Yes, we thank you. A while ago, you said something to Chance I've wanted to address about allowing her to sing. I'll never be threatened by my wife's anointing and gifts. She's a powerhouse and every time I see her doing what God has ordained, I'm proud. I also love to hear her hit them high notes. All of them, if you know what I mean."

Mason comes over and pulls me into his arms, kissing me on the lips. When he releases me, we look back to see Jeff is gone. We burst into laughing.

❊❊❊❊❊

A week later, I'm walking out of a coffee shop when I bump into Olivia, my sister-in-law.

"Chance, hey. It's been a while," she states.

"It has. How are you?"

"I'm great. Cameron and I are expecting our first baby."

"Congratulations. I pray you'll have a successful pregnancy."

"Wait, your brother is here."

"Okay," I say like it's supposed to mean something.

"He misses you."

"Well, my number hasn't changed. Good luck to you both."

"Chance, wait."

I sigh and turn back to see Cameron rushing up. "What's up?"

"Can I buy you a coffee and we chat for a moment?"

I raise the cup in my hand.

"Right, my bad. Can we talk?" he asks.

"I'll be inside," Olivia says.

"I'm sorry Chance. I've allowed all these months to pass without reaching out to you. I've been meaning too but then I chicken out. It's no excuse," he says when I open my mouth to say something. "I'm a grown man who shouldn't be allowing my mother to dictate the relationship with my big sister. I'm sorry."

"Cameron, thank you for apologizing and congratulations on the baby. However, I've moved on and the only thing I'm sorry about is the fact we don't have a relationship. You're my baby brother who's about to become a father and your stupidity is stopping me from enjoying that. Yet, it's your cross to bear. I wish you and Olivia nothing but happiness, and I mean it."

"Can we start over?"

"What's with this starting over crap? Cameron, this isn't a game of connect four that you're losing at. This is life and there are no do overs. Yes, we can move forward but the damage has been done and we both know, you aren't going to go against your mother. I forgive you though." I start to walk off.

"I'm in therapy," he blurts, and I stop. "I started going after Jamaica and at first, it was to make Olivia happy but somewhere along the way it began to do something inwardly. Chance, I'm thirty-six and about to become a dad. I can't go on like this. Two days ago, I told mom I was reaching out to you to recover our relationship and let's just say, she didn't take it well. That's her problem. Big sister, I've missed out on having you in my life and I don't want to anymore. I want my son to know who his auntie is. I want him to get mad at me, call you and you come running.

I want you to buy him what his mom and I said he couldn't have. I want you to be a constant in his life, so he'll know he can depend on you. I want you to be the next best thing besides his mom. I want you to sing to him like you used to do me when I was six and having bad dreams. Heck, I want to call you when I'm having a bad day and you talk me through it. I need my big sister and I'm sorry it's taken me this long to realize it. Please forgive me and give me another chance."

I look at him as tears spill down his face.

"Please," he whispers.

I close the gap between us giving him a hug and he sobs.

"I'm so sorry," he cries.

"I forgive you."

He squeezes me tighter.

Chapter 23

Over the next few weeks, Cameron and I spend more time together. He, Olivia and dad have been to the house a few times for dinner and church for Sunday service. I was shocked when they all decided to join. Dad's divorce was final last week, and he's excited to make things official with Ms. Sheryl from the church. Cameron tried to set up a meeting with us and Taylor, but she refused like I knew she would.

Today, Mason, Marcy, dad and I are having dinner and Cameron's house to celebrate his birthday. His is a week before mine. Ringing the doorbell, Olivia lets me in. Mason is in the car finishing a call with Mother Tate who is very long winded. Marcy text to say she'll be pulling up in a few minutes. Walking into the living room, I stop when I see mom and Taylor.

"Well, well if it isn't the prodigal daughter," Taylor gripes.

"Chance, I thought you'd fallen off the face of the earth," Mom adds. "How have you been?"

"I've been great. You?"

"We're great. You're looking well," she says like it's painful.

I chuckle. "I am. Olivia, is there anything I can help you with?"

"No, we have a chef tonight who has everything covered. As soon as everyone else arrives we can move to the dining room."

"Why are you in a rush to end our conversation dear sister?" Taylor asks. "Don't want me to ask the whereabouts of your new boyfriend? I know you have one because you can never go long without a man to use you, I mean be with you." She laughs.

"Says the one who's single. How's the divorce coming along?"

Her face turns red. "At least I have a husband."

"Had," I correct, "because from the looks of Travis' IG, he's doing very well with his new thick boo."

Mason walks in with Marcy and my dad.

"Arthur, what are you doing here?" mom angrily asks as Cameron and Olivia join us. "Did you invite him?" she turns to Cameron.

"Yes, mom I did. It's my birthday and I wanted my family to celebrate with me."

"Family?" she hisses.

"Family," my dad repeats with a huge smile. "This is my ex-wife Camilla and my daughter Taylor. This is Sheryl, my woman and this is Chance's husband Pastor Mason Gray and Marcy—"

"Her daughter," Marcy cuts in. "It's nice to meet all of you."

Mom's face looks like all the blood is draining from it.

"Your what?" Taylor exclaims. "You're married?"

"I am. Now, are we having dinner or not."

We walk into the dining room leaving Taylor and mom standing there. After a few minutes, they decide to join us. The first twenty minutes, during appetizers they kept making snide remarks amongst themselves until Cameron shut them down. He told them to respect the table or leave.

They hushed themselves really quick.

"Sheryl, what do you do?" mom questions.

"I'm a pediatric doctor," she answers.

"She's going to be the baby's doctor," Cameron adds. "We were so lucky to have met her."

"Oh," mom stiffens. "How did you all meet?"

"At church."

"Church?" Taylor chuckles. "Arthur goes to church?"

"I'm still your dad," he says to her and she rolls her eyes.

"Yes, we all do," Cameron tells her. "We became members of Harvest Tabernacle of Praise where Chance and Mason serve about three weeks ago."

"You all should visit us sometimes," I throw in. "You may find that Jesus is forgiving and welcoming in spite of what you do."

"What is that supposed to mean?" mom inquires dropping her fork.

I shrug. "Just what it insinuates."

"Little girl—"

"I'm a grown woman Camilla," I assert, "and save the tantrum for some other time, preferably when I'm not around because we've all heard it and it's old."

"Child, are you still caught up on what I said in Jamaica? It was the truth and sorry if it hurt."

"It doesn't," I assure her, "not anymore."

"It must if you keep bringing it up. Look, I apologize for not being the mother you desired but I am who I am. Take me or leave me."

"I didn't bring it up, you did but I choose the latter."

"What?"

"I choose to leave you as you are. Mother, it's not for me to change you and from the sound of things, you're not wanting too. I love and respect you because you are my mother, although it wasn't my choice but that's all you're getting from me. I will not waste anymore good energy fighting or arguing with you nor will I seek your affection or love. It's obvious you can't give it to me and I'm good with that because everything I thought I missed God has restored and all I needed, God provides. Whatever you did or didn't do, no longer keeps me up at night. I've forgiven you and Taylor and moved on. It's time you two did the same."

"And who are you supposed to be? Some Dalai Lama with inspirational wisdom," Taylor bellows. "You think I care about your forgiveness because you've found Jesus? A few months ago, you were a pitiful being who'd been dumped by yet another man, crying because your half naked pictures were all over the internet and—"

"Is that all you got sis because I'm not that person anymore. The narrative you know is old and no longer bothers me. My past deeds don't define me, but they refined me so allow me to reintroduce myself. My name is Chance Alondra Gray, happy wife, mother, daughter, sister and First Lady of a church. I'm an anointed being who can sing, pray, lay hands and speak in tongue. I can also build and keep a home and job while tending to my husband's mental, emotional and physical needs."

"Very good might I add," Mason says, and I smile.

"Sis, while you may not think you need my forgiveness, you do, and you have it. However, that old story was good but not my best. Next time you tell it, edit it to include my come up."

"Um damn," Olivia says. "I was going to say dinner is served but shoot."

"Babe, I'm proud of you," Mason says when we're on our way home. "The way you handled your mom and sister tonight."

"Thank you. I meant what I said. Their antics don't bother me anymore. They are the ones whose life will be miserable without family, I have mine."

Chapter 24

"Babe are you ready," Mason asks for the fifth time. "Woman, if you don't come on, we're going to be late."

We're in Jamaica to celebrate my birthday and the first anniversary of us meeting.

"I'm ready," I reply opening the door to the bathroom.

"Good God. Nah, we ain't going."

I laugh.

I run my hand down the front of me. "Too much?" I refer to the white, one shoulder jumpsuit that's hugging every curve. My locs are up in a tight knot, long dangling earrings, mascara hitting and burgundy lipstick popping.

"You look amazing. Wait, I need to capture this moment." He pulls out his phone and I pose. "Okay, let's go before I change my mind."

"Are you going to finally tell me where we're going?"

"Nope."

We get downstairs and a car is waiting. After driving for a while, the car stops. The driver opens the door and we're at the same harbor from a year ago.

"Babe," I say getting emotional.

"I wanted this trip to be even better than before."

He grabs my hand and we walk the short distance.

"Good evening Mr. and Mrs. Gray. Welcome aboard."

"Good evening sir," Mason replies.

"We'll be setting sail in about twenty minutes. For now, you can enjoy the appetizers set up for you."

Thirty minutes later, we're led to the dining room.

"Oh my God," I squeal when I see the burgundy and white balloons and white roses that fill the room.

"Happy Birthday my love."

I wrap my arms around him. "Thank you."

He releases me and hands me a box. I open it to see a pandora bracelet filled with charms.

"Each of these have special meanings," he says and of course I'm crying. "This family tree represents us, a happy birthday because it's your day, a love coupon that you can always redeem with me, a cross for God, my beautiful wife charm is self-explanatory, this 40th celebration charm will always remind you of when we met and a music note for you finding your voice again. This final charm, is called a bow and heart charm and it represents the password to your heart, love. What you're been yearning for all along."

"Mason," I cry throwing my arms around him. "Baby, thank you."

"Everything for you."

"I love you," I tell him.

"I love you too."

For the next hour, we enjoy a full course meal and like before it was amazing. Dessert was my favorite, red velvet cheesecake. Walking to the main deck, he goes over to a speaker, connects his phone and when the music begins, I smile. The Staple Singers.

"Let me take you there," he sings holding out his hand to me.

I dance over to him joining in. "I know a place y'all," we both say.

We continue to dance together until I motion for the young lady to switch it. The music changes to a song by Baby Face called The Day.

"Wait, let me change the song. I don't know what that is," he says looking confused.

I grab his hand and begin to sing changing some of the lyrics.

"It was late October the news came, and I got excited, I cried all day. And you were such a lovely, precious sight when I saw our baby in your eyes. It was like falling deep in love. I heard the angels cry above. I felt a blessing straight from God the day you gave me a child. I called about everyone I knew. Just think, I'll be a mother because of you. There's no greater love than what you gave, a brand-new baby on the way."

He doesn't take his eyes off of me as the young lady hands him a box.

"Babe, open it."

He opens it to find a onesie that says, you're going to be a daddy and the ultrasound picture.

"You're pregnant?"

"Yes," I say with tears falling. "I found out about four weeks ago and knew I wanted to tell you here where it all started for us. It was so hard keeping it a secret."

He grabs my face. "You're having my baby?"

"June 13, 2021."

"Yes," he screams. "Wait, so you knew my plan the entire time?"

"Well," I shrug. "You left your email up with the confirmation, so I called and made a few changes."

"Chance, another chance," he repeats. "Girl, I love you."

"I love you too."

THE END

Thank you for taking the time to read and support Another Chance. I pray you've enjoyed getting to know Chance McGhee. If you did, please leave a review and tell someone about it.

Although this book is fictional, the message of God still remains ... you too are given Another Chance. Whether it be love, business, school, starting over, etc.; you have **ANOTHER CHANCE** every time you open your eyes. Don't take it for granted.

As always, I'm grateful each time you support me. If this is your first or twentieth time reading a book by me, THANK YOU! If we haven't connected on social media or through text, what are you waiting for.

Please check out the many other books available by visiting my Amazon Page. For upcoming contests and give-a-ways, I invite you to like my Facebook page, AuthorLakisha, join my reading group Twins Write 2 or follow https://authorlakishajohnson.com/. You can also text LJBOOKS to 31996 to be kept up to date on all things, Lakisha, the Author.

Or you can connect with me on Social Media.

Twitter: _kishajohnson

Instagram: kishajohnson and DearSisVlog

Snapchat: Authorlakisha

Tik Tok: Author Lakisha

Email: authorlakisha@gmail.com

About the Author

Lakisha has been writing since 2012 and has penned more than twenty-five novels, devotionals and journals. You can find topics of faith, abuse, marriage, love, loss, grief, losing hope etc. on the pages of her many books.

In addition to being a self-published author, she's also a wife of 22 years, mother of 2, Co-Pastor of Macedonia MB Church in Hollywood, MS; Sr. Business Analyst with FedEx, Devotional Blogger, the product of a large family. She's a college graduate with 2 Associate Degrees in IT and a Bachelor of Science in Bible.

Lakisha writes from her heart and doesn't take the credit for what God does because if you were to strip away everything; you'd see that Lakisha is simply a woman who boldly, unapologetically and gladly loves and works for God.

Ask her and she'll tell you, "It's not just writing, its ministry."

Also available

When the Vows Break

Dearly beloved, that's how it begins, what God has joined together, let no man put asunder; that's how it ends. Happily married, wedded bliss and with these rings, we do take; but what happens to happily ever after when the vows break?

Secrets, lying, cheating, drugs, alcohol and temptations prove that not everything is what it seems.

Will the chaos of it all be more than they can take? Find out in part 1 of When the Vows Break

https://www.amazon.com/dp/B07V7139BW

Broken

Gwendolyn was 13 when her dad shattered her heart, leaving her broken. Her mother told her, a daddy can break a girl's heart before any man has a chance and she was right. Through many failed relationships and giving herself to any man who showed interest, she knew she had to get herself together. So, she gave up on men.

Until Jacque. He came into her life with promises to love, honor and cherish her; forsaking all others until death do, they part. Twelve years later, he has made good on his promises until he didn't.

https://www.amazon.com/dp/B07QZCW9ZX

The Family that Lies:

Forsaken by Grayce, Saved by Merci

Born only months apart, Merci and Grayce Alexander were as close as sisters could get. With a father who thought the world of them, life was good. Until one day everything changed.

While Grayce got love and attention, Merci got all the hell, forcing her to leave home. She never looks back, putting the past behind her until her sister shows up over a decade later begging for help, bringing all of the forgotten past with her. Yes, every family has their secrets, hidden truths and ties but Merci had no idea she'd been born into the family that lies.

https://www.amazon.com/dp/B01MAZD49X

The Pastor's Admin

Daphne 'Dee' Gary used to love being an admin … until Joseph Thornton. She has been his administrative assistant for ten years and each year, she has to decide whether it will be his secrets or her sanity. And the choice is beginning to take a toil.

Daphne knows life can be hard and flesh will sometimes win but when she has to choose between HIS SECRETS or HER SANITY, this time, will she remain The Pastor's Admin?

https://www.amazon.com/dp/B07B9V4981

The Marriage Bed

Lynn and Jerome Watson have been together since meeting in the halls of Booker T. Washington High School, in 1993. Twenty-five years, a house, business and three children later they are on the heels of their 18th wedding anniversary and Lynn's 40th birthday. Her only request ... a night of fun at home with her husband and maybe a few toys.

Lynn thinks their marriage bed is suffering. Jerome, on the other hand, thinks Lynn is overreacting. His thoughts, if it ain't broke, don't break it trying to fix it. Then something happens that shakes up the Watson household and secrets are revealed but the biggest secret, Jerome has, and his lips are sealed.

https://www.amazon.com/dp/B07H51VS45

Still Fighting:

My sister's fight with Trigeminal Neuralgia

What would you do if you woke up one morning with pain doctors couldn't diagnose, medicine couldn't minimize, sleep couldn't stop and kept getting worse?

Still Fighting is an inside look into my sister's continued fight with Trigeminal Neuralgia, a condition known as the Suicide Disease because of the lives it has taken. In this book, I take you on a journey of recognition, route and restoration from my point of view; a sister who would stop at nothing to help her twin sister/best friend fight to live.

https://www.amazon.com/dp/B07MJHF6NL

The Forgotten Wife

All Rylee wants is her husband's attention. She used to be the apple of Todd's eye but no matter what she did, lately, he was just too busy to notice her. She could not help but wonder why.

They say first comes love then comes ... a kidnapping, attacks, lies and affairs. Someone is out for blood but who, what, when and why?

Secrets are revealed and Rylee fears for her life when all she ever wanted was not to be The Forgotten Wife.

https://www.amazon.com/gp/product/B07DRQ8NPR

Other Available Titles

A Compilation of Christian Stories: Box Set

Shattered Vows Box Set

Dear God: Hear My Prayer

2:32 AM: Losing My Faith in God

When the Vows Break 2

When the Vows Break 3

Shattered

Shattered 2

Tense

Last Call

Covet

I'm Not Crazy

Infidelity

Bible Chicks: Book 2

Doses of Devotion

You Only Live Once: Youth Devotional

HERoine Addict – Journal

Be A Fighter - Journal

Surviving Me - Journal

www.ingramcontent.com/pod-product-compliance
Lightning Source LLC
Chambersburg PA
CBHW071503140726
47997CB00005B/1843